The intruder had go ☑ **P9-ELQ-592**
last night that she hadn't even heard him
until Connor had cried out. Was he out
there now?

Watching?

And what would he do about Forrest being here again?
Over his staying to search the house?

Would he make good on his threat?

Tears rushed to her eyes, and she blinked furiously as
she turned away. But Forrest must have seen them—
because he caught her arm, the one from which Connor's
car carrier swung. He turned her back toward him.

"Are you okay?" he asked, his deep voice even deeper
with concern.

Rae closed her eyes and willed the tears away. "I..."
She couldn't tell him.

As if he'd read her mind, he implored her, "You can tell
me."

But she shook her head. "I have to go." She jerked
away from him and rushed toward her small SUV.
Hopefully her intruder had seen that and realized she
was doing everything she could to get rid of Forrest.

Unless...

Unless he didn't just want the detective to go away.
Maybe he wanted him dead.

* * *

Dear Reader,

I'm so honored to have been invited to participate in another Colton continuity. Colton 911 is as exciting as it sounds, and I loved writing my contribution to the series—*Colton 911: Baby's Bodyguard*.

Bodies keep turning up in Whisperwood, Texas—some old, some new and not all because of the hurricane that recently hit the area. The Coltons who work with the Cowboy Heroes, a horseback rescue agency, wind up staying in their hometown to help with the aftermath of the hurricane and to figure out who's responsible for the deaths not attributed to the hurricane.

Forrest Colton was once a hotshot Austin cold case detective—until a gunshot wound permanently disabled him. Forrest volunteers with the Cowboy Heroes but finds himself enlisted to help Whisperwood PD solve the murders. He's glad he's taken on the case when he personally finds a body in the backyard of beautiful Rae Lemmon. The single mom is too busy with her baby boy, her paralegal job and law school to fall for any man, especially one as surly as Forrest. But murder, threats, family and friends keep throwing them together until they don't know if they're trying to escape a killer or their attraction for each other.

I hope you enjoy this book as much as I enjoyed writing it!

Happy reading!

Lisa Childs

COLTON 911: BABY'S BODYGUARD

Lisa Childs

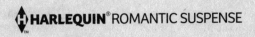
HARLEQUIN® ROMANTIC SUSPENSE

Special thanks and acknowledgment are given to Lisa Childs
for her contribution to the Colton 911 miniseries.

Recycling programs
for this product may
not exist in your area.

ISBN-13: 978-1-335-66210-1

Colton 911: Baby's Bodyguard

Copyright © 2019 by Harlequin Books S.A.

Printed in U.S.A.

Ever since **Lisa Childs** read her first romance novel (a Harlequin story, of course) at age eleven, all she wanted was to be a romance writer. With over forty novels published with Harlequin, Lisa is living her dream. She is an award-winning, bestselling romance author. Lisa loves to hear from readers, who can contact her on Facebook, through her website, lisachilds.com, or her snail-mail address, PO Box 139, Marne, MI 49435.

Books by Lisa Childs

Harlequin Romantic Suspense

Colton 911

Colton 911: Baby's Bodyguard

Bachelor Bodyguards

His Christmas Assignment
Bodyguard Daddy
Bodyguard's Baby Surprise
Beauty and the Bodyguard
Nanny Bodyguard
Single Mom's Bodyguard
In the Bodyguard's Arms
Soldier Bodyguard
Guarding His Witness

The Coltons of Red Ridge

Colton's Cinderella Bride

Top Secret Deliveries

The Bounty Hunter's Baby Surprise

The Coltons of Shadow Creek

The Colton Marine

Visit the Author Profile page at Harlequin.com for more titles.

For Marie Ferrarella, Carla Cassidy and
Beth Cornelison—it was an honor to work on this
Colton series with such amazing authors!

Chapter 1

Her eyes were wide with fear and death. She stared up at him as if appealing to him for help. She wasn't the only one.

"Come on, Forrest," his brother Donovan implored him. "Whisperwood PD needs your expertise."

Forrest gestured at the body lying amid the piles of dirt where Lone Star Pharma had intended to expand its parking lot. The drug company had had to put its plans on hold once the asphalt crew had dug up the body. "This isn't a cold case."

She couldn't have been buried that long; the body had barely begun decomp. Not that he was that close to the scene, which the techs were still processing. He'd wanted to stay out of the way, but his brothers had urged him closer.

"This isn't the only body that turned up recently," Jonah, the oldest of his brothers, chimed in on the conversation. He and Donovan had picked up Forrest from their parents' ranch and brought him out here. Now he understood why. They were trying to get him involved in the investigation.

They stared at him now. And even though Donovan wasn't biologically their brother, he looked more like Jonah than any of their biological brothers did. They were both dark haired and dark eyed, whereas Forrest's hair was lighter brown and longer than their buzz cuts, and his eyes were hazel.

"Unfortunately she isn't the only recent casualty," Forrest agreed.

A dozen people had lost their lives due to the flooding and wind damage Hurricane Brooke had wreaked on Whisperwood, Texas. Despite being early in the season, the storm had been deadly.

"That's why we're here—to help out because of the natural disaster," he reminded his brothers. They were part of the Cowboy Heroes, a horseback rescue organization formed years ago by ranchers and EMTs. Forrest had volunteered to help the Heroes' search-and-recovery efforts—not the police department. "And this isn't a natural disaster."

Though this person might have been one of the people reported missing since the hurricane, the storm hadn't caused her death. From what Forrest could see in the lights that the Whisperwood PD's forensic unit had set up to illuminate the crime scene, the young woman had bruising around her neck and on her arms and legs. She hadn't drowned or been struck by a fallen tree.

She'd probably been strangled and maybe worse.

A chill raced down his spine despite the warmth of the August night. The death had happened recently.

"This is murder," Jonah said. He must have noticed what Forrest had. "Just like the body that Maggie and I found last month." He shuddered now. "And that one definitely falls within your area of expertise."

Forrest shook his head. "Not anymore."

A shooting had forced his early retirement from the Austin Police Department's cold-case unit. That shooting and the pins that held together the shattered bones in his leg were why he'd had to retire with disability and why, as a volunteer with the Cowboy Heroes, he was consigned to a desk, operating the telephones. He took the calls about what people were missing: loved ones and livestock. But he'd rather be out in the field with his brothers, actually searching for those missing people and animals. Hell, he'd rather be back on the job. And they knew him so damn well that they were aware of that.

Jonah lowered his voice to a gruff whisper and murmured, "Not because you don't want to."

Sure, he would love to go back to the job, but there was no way in hell that he could pass a physical now. Not with his leg.

As if he'd read Forrest's mind, Jonah continued, "But you can now. The chief will give you a special dispensation to help out as an interim detective."

The "special dispensation" pricked his pride, and

he clenched his jaw. "I don't need you all doing me any favors."

"You'd be doing me the favor," Donovan said. "I was just about to leave on my honeymoon when this call came into the department." Donovan helped out only part-time with the Cowboy Heroes; he was a full-time K9 cop with Whisperwood PD.

"It's a mini honeymoon," Forrest reminded him. "You're not going to be gone long."

"But even when we get back, I'm going to be distracted," Donovan claimed. "Bellamy's pregnant."

Jonah chortled and slapped their brother's back. "That's great! That's wonderful news."

And with everything that had happened since the hurricane, good news was more than welcome.

"Congratulations," Forrest said, and he reached out and squeezed his brother's shoulder. Donovan and Bellamy so deserved their happiness. They'd been through so much recently.

"Thanks," Donovan said with a big grin. But then he glanced down at the body and shook his head. "She deserves someone's full attention, and the police department and the chief are just stretched too damn thin right now, dealing with the aftermath of the hurricane."

And the other dead body.

The chief's sister. Had someone else really murdered her? Or was serial killer Elliot Corgan messing with everyone from beyond his grave?

Forrest wouldn't put it past the sadistic son of a bitch. When he'd been on the job, he'd dealt with quite a few serial killers. They got nearly as much enjoyment playing mind games with law enforcement as they did killing.

He glanced down at the dead girl. At least one thing was for certain: Elliot hadn't killed her. He wouldn't have been able to manage that from beyond the grave. Unless…

"You're already on the case," Jonah said with a slight smile. "I can see your wheels turning."

Forrest glared at his big brother, but he didn't deny it. Too many thoughts flitted through his mind. Was she one of the people presumed missing because of Hurricane Brooke? Had someone taken advantage of the storm to murder her, thinking that law enforcement would assume she'd been lost in the flooding that had followed the storm?

Chief Thompson had been moving around the crime scene, talking to the techs and officers guarding the perimeter. Ignoring the reporters who shouted questions at him from the other side of the police tape, Whisperwood PD's top cop walked toward Forrest and his brothers. Thompson had been doing this job for a long time, and his experience showed in the lines in his face and the way his shoulders sagged when he looked down at the body. He shook his head and sighed, and his Stetson slipped lower over his face.

Forrest had realized some years into his career that it would never get any easier to see someone dead, especially *murdered*, and the chief just proved that to him. He let his own hat slide down to shield his face.

Thompson turned away from the body to focus on Forrest now, his blue eyes sharp with intelligence and determination. "So, you going to do it? You going to take the job?"

His brothers stared at him, nodding and smiling to encourage his acceptance. They probably figured this would be good for him, would get him back doing the job he loved. But when he'd been shot, the job hadn't been the only thing he'd lost that he loved.

That experience had taught him never to risk his heart again. So the job was all he had—even if it was just a short-term assignment.

He nodded. "Yes, I'll take it."

Not for his sake, though, like his brothers obviously wanted. But for hers.

He stared down at the dead woman, determined to make sure she got the justice she deserved and that the killer would not hurt anyone else.

"He's so cute," Bellamy cooed as she cradled the baby against her chest and kissed the top of his head. He'd been born with a full head of soft brown hair, the same chocolaty color as his mama's. He also had her big brown eyes.

Rae's heart swelled with maternal pride. "Yes, he is," she said just as a yawn slipped out. He'd also been keeping her up nights with a bout of colic, and Bellamy's bed was so comfy, Rae was tempted to take a nap right there amid the pile of clothes and the suitcase.

"Hey, you need to finish packing," Maggie told her sister as she pried the baby from Bellamy's arms. "You're supposed to be leaving for your honeymoon."

"I will," Bellamy said. "As soon as Donovan gets back from the crime scene."

Rae shuddered. "So another body's been found?" Twelve people had died in the hurricane, but she'd thought all of the missing had been accounted for— thanks to the Cowboy Heroes' rescue-and-recovery efforts.

Maggie had been one of the missing. Fortunately she had been found alive. Jonah Colton hadn't just rescued her, though; he'd also fallen in love with the former beauty queen. A pang of wistfulness tugged at Rae's heart, not that she wanted anyone falling in love with her.

She was too busy with her two-month-old son and her law-school classes and her new job as a paralegal to fit a man into her life right now. Or ever.

Connor was the only man for her. She smiled as he clutched his fingers around a lock of Maggie's pretty blond hair. Like every other male in Whisperwood, he was drawn to the former beauty queen.

Rae might have been jealous if Maggie wasn't as beautiful inside as she was on the outside. She twisted her pretty features into comical faces as she cooed at the fascinated baby. Then she glanced up at Rae and a frown pulled down the corners of her mouth. "From what the chief told Jonah, it sounds like the death had nothing to do with the hurricane."

Rae gasped. "Was it…like the body you and Jonah found?"

Maggie shuddered. "I hope not."

That body had been mummified. Rae hadn't seen

it, but just the thought of it had given her nightmares. She couldn't imagine what Maggie had gone through because of that and the threats to her life.

All of the crime in Whisperwood was what had compelled Rae to take the LSAT to try to get into law school. Nobody had probably been as surprised as she'd been that she'd done so well that she'd had her pick of schools. Of course she'd chosen to stay in Whisperwood with her friends. With her mom gone, they were the only family she had now—except for Connor. She'd already been pregnant with him when she'd taken the exam.

Bellamy nipped her bottom lip with her teeth. "Maybe Donovan and I shouldn't go away right now."

"No!" Rae and Maggie both shouted.

Connor, startled, began to cry. Rae jumped up from the bed and took him from Maggie. Holding him close, she rubbed her hand up and down his back and murmured, "It's okay, sweetheart. You're okay."

He settled down with a hiccuping sob. Then the tension drained from his tiny body and he began to drift off to sleep like Rae had longed to.

"You're so good with him," Maggie said with a smile.

"You are," Bellamy agreed. She looked more like Rae, with dark hair and eyes, and with as long as they'd known each other, they were more like sisters than friends. "You're amazing. I can't believe how much you're doing all on your own."

Rae smiled with pleasure and pride. But then she reminded her friend, "You've done the same."

Maggie's mouth pulled down into another frown, and regret struck a pang in Rae's heart. She hadn't meant to cause any issues between the sisters. They'd already had too many.

"I was never alone," Bellamy said. "I had you, Rae." She turned toward Maggie and smiled at her sister. "And you… I just didn't realize what all you were doing for me."

"Rae's right," Maggie said. "You did all the heavy lifting on your own." Taking care of their ailing parents. "You deserve this honeymoon. You deserve every happiness. Don't let Donovan back out of going."

Bellamy smiled. "Not a chance. He's determined to go. He and Jonah are going to work on convincing Forrest to step in and take over the murder investigations."

Maggie nodded. "Oh, that's what big brother is up to." She'd fallen for the oldest of the Colton brothers. "He said he was going to pick up Forrest."

Another little pang struck Rae's heart at the mention of that particular Colton brother. It was probably just regret again. She shouldn't have asked him to dance at Bellamy and Donovan's wedding. But as one of two maids of honor, she'd wanted to make sure every guest enjoyed the celebration. That was the only reason she'd asked—not because he was ridiculously good-looking, with his chiseled features and his brooding intensity.

He hadn't had to be so curt with her, though. Sure, she'd known he had a limp from an injury in the line of duty. But he still worked with the Cowboy Heroes, so she hadn't thought he was really disabled. He could have held her and just swayed from side to side. It wasn't as if she'd asked him to two-step or line dance with her. But she shouldn't have asked at all. The only reason she had was because of how alone he'd looked... even among all of his family.

And that loneliness had called to hers. Because even with her son and her good friends, she sometimes felt alone like that, too. That was better, though, than falling for someone only to have him leave.

"I didn't think Forrest was going to stick around much longer," she said. "Won't he move on to the next natural disaster, with the rest of the Cowboy Heroes?"

"Whisperwood needs them for more than rescue-and-recovery efforts right now," Maggie said. She shuddered again. "There's a killer on the loose."

"That's why we should postpone our honeymoon," Bellamy said.

"No," Rae and Maggie said again, their voices soft this time, though.

Bellamy sighed. "Okay, but you both need to promise me that you'll be extra careful."

"Of course," they agreed, again in unison.

"I know Jonah won't let anything happen to you," Bellamy told her sister. "But you..."

Rae smiled. "I can take care of myself." She'd done it for most of her life.

Bellamy took the sleeping baby from her arms and snuggled him against her. "But you have Connor to worry about, too, and your classes. I'm really concerned about you living out there in the country, alone."

"I'm not alone," Rae reminded her.

Bellamy pressed another kiss to the soft hair on Connor's head. "He's not going to be much protection against a bad guy—at least not for a few more years."

"Like twenty," Maggie added with a chuckle.

"I don't need a man to protect me," Rae said. She'd never had one. Her father had been more likely to put her and her mother in danger—at least financially— than to protect them. "I don't need a man at all."

"You proved that by having this little guy on your own," Maggie said. "I admire you."

"Me, too," Bellamy added. "Although I think I had more fun conceiving mine the way we did."

Rae stared at her friend. "What?"

"I'm pregnant," the new bride announced, her face glowing with happiness and love.

Tears rushed to Rae's eyes. "That's wonderful."

"So wonderful," Maggie agreed as her eyes filled with tears, too. "I'm thrilled for you."

"Me, too," Rae said. "You and Donovan are going to be amazing parents."

"I'm going to drive you crazy," Bellamy warned her, "with all the questions I'll be asking you." Bellamy's mom was gone, like Rae's was.

Rae missed her mom every day. They'd been so close; Georgia had been more of a friend than a mother to her. Now that she was a mother herself, she'd never needed her more.

"You won't drive me crazy at all," Rae assured her. "I'm not sure I'll have all the answers, though." Mostly she felt as if she was stumbling around in the dark, blindly finding her way as a parent and as a student again at thirty-five.

"You'll have more than I'll have," Maggie said. "You're the smartest, most independent person I know."

The tears already stinging her eyes threatened to spill over, but Rae blinked them back to smile at her friend. "I'm not sure about smartest. Law school is tougher than I thought it would be."

"Because you just had a baby two months ago and you're working," Bellamy reminded her as she stared down at Connor, who was sleeping so peacefully in her arms.

If only he slept that peacefully at night...

"It'll get easier," Rae said. That was what she kept telling herself.

Bellamy chuckled softly. "You're smart, but I think it's your stubbornness that keeps you going."

A smile tugged at the corners of Rae's mouth. She couldn't deny that.

"Just don't be so stubborn and independent that you put yourself in danger," Bellamy advised. "Promise?"

Rae sighed. "Of course I'm not going to put myself or Connor in danger," she assured her. "Stop worrying about me. And let's get you ready for your honeymoon!"

"Since she's already pregnant, I think she knows about the birds and the bees," Maggie teased.

They all laughed, rousing Connor from his impromptu nap. But he didn't cry when he awakened; he just groggily looked up at Bellamy, who was holding him. She was like an aunt to him, and Maggie was fast becoming like another. These women and her baby were the only family that Rae needed.

She didn't need a man for protection or for anything else. But when she left Bellamy's cute two-bedroom house and headed home with Connor safely buckled into the back seat, an odd chill passed through her despite the warmth of the August night. Fear.

Maybe it was all of the talk about bodies and killers.

Or maybe it was her postpartum hormones.

She preferred to blame the hormones. Because she had nothing to fear.

The television screen illuminated only the area of the dark room around the TV. From the shadows, he watched the evening news report from the crime scene at Lone Star Pharma.

Her body had been found. His hands clenched into fists as rage coursed through him.

Damn it...

The news crews had been kept back, behind the police barricade. But the camera zoomed in on the scene and captured the people investigating the discovery. The Cowboy Heroes.

What the hell were they doing there?

He unclenched one fist to turn the volume up.

"Chief Thompson has enlisted the help of former Austin cold-case detective Forrest Colton," the reporter announced. "Colton has been given special dispensation from the Whisperwood Police Department to lead the investigation of this murder and the body discovered last month in a mummified condition. Colton holds the highest clearance rate in the Austin Police Department, so an arrest seems imminent."

He cursed again.

No. An arrest was not imminent. Forrest Colton might have gotten lucky in Austin, but his luck was about to run out in Whisperwood. And maybe his life, as well.

Chapter 2

A week had passed since his brothers had ambushed him at the crime scene. A week of frustration that gripped Forrest so intensely, he wished he'd never accepted the position no matter how temporary it was going to be.

The hurricane had caused so much damage, and not just physically. Emotionally people were dealing with the loss of loved ones and their homes or their livelihoods. The Whisperwood Police Department was stretched thin. The crime-scene techs were understaffed and overworked, so nothing had been processed yet from either scene. And the coroner...

She hadn't even taken the bodies from their refrigerated drawers yet, let alone begun the autopsies. And until he had more information, Forrest didn't want to parade in the family members of every missing person to see if the dead woman was their loved one. He didn't want to put every family that was missing someone through that kind of pain.

Hell, he didn't want to put one family through that kind of pain. But it was inevitable. Once they figured out who she was.

Everybody expected miracles from Forrest, but his hands were nearly as tied as the poor victim's hands had been—bound behind her back.

He wrapped the reins around his hands and clenched his knees together as the quarter horse he rode scrambled over the uneven ground. Despite taking the detective position, Forrest continued as a volunteer for the Cowboy Heroes. The team was not done with Whisperwood and the surrounding area, which had been hit particularly hard with flooding after Hurricane Brooke.

The water had begun to recede, though, leaving only muddy areas like the one in which the horse's hooves now slipped. His mount leaning, Forrest nearly slipped off it and into the mud. Ignoring the twinge of pain in his bad leg, he tightened his grip.

"Whoa, steady," Forrest murmured soothingly. When the horse regained its balance, a sigh of relief slipped through Forrest's lips. This was why he usually handled the desk work for the rescue agency and not the fieldwork. But like his brothers, he'd been born in the saddle. He couldn't *not* ride.

He wasn't able to help with the rescues as physically as he would have liked, though. Sometimes his leg wouldn't hold his weight, let alone the weight of another person or animal. He sighed again but this time with resignation. It was what it was.

He'd accepted that a while ago. And he helped out where he could—like riding around to survey the areas. There were still some people missing, and maybe the floodwater had hidden their remains.

Not that he wanted to find any more bodies.

But that was the purpose of the recovery part of the Cowboy Heroes' rescue-and-recovery operation. Survivors needed that closure of knowing what had happened to their loved one and having that body to bury. That was why he needed the body in the morgue identified, so he could give her family some small measure of peace.

Until he found her killer.

And he would.

His frustration turning back to determination, he urged the horse across the muddy stretch of land. Heat shimmered off the black shingles of a roof in the distance. He'd started out early from his family ranch, before the sun had even risen much above the horizon, and it wasn't much higher now. So it was going to be another hot August day, which was good.

The last of the water should recede and reveal whatever secrets it has been hiding. Whatever bodies...of animals and people.

So much livestock had been lost, too. A pang of regret over all of those losses struck his heart. Then another pang of regret struck him when he realized whose house he'd come upon in the country.

Hers.

Rae Lemmon. His new sister-in-law's best friend,

and quite the beauty. He hadn't lived in Whisperwood for years, but he remembered this was her family home. And maybe he'd subconsciously headed that way.

But why? Sure, she was beautiful, but because she was beautiful, she wouldn't want anything to do with a disabled man. She'd asked him to dance at the wedding, but that must have only been out of pity or maybe just a sense of obligation to her friend.

And maybe that was why he'd come this way, to check on her place—out of a sense of obligation. She was his new sister-in-law's best friend, so that almost made her family, too. And as much as the Coltons took care of everyone else, they took extra care of their own.

He knew that because of how everybody had taken care of him after he'd been shot. Well, everybody but one person. But she hadn't been family yet, and after he'd been shot, she'd returned his ring.

He flinched as the memory rushed over him. Not that he could blame her. As she'd said, she hadn't fallen in love with a cripple, so he really shouldn't have expected her to stick around for him. It wasn't as if they'd said their vows yet either, and now he expected those vows would not have included "in sickness and in health."

While the old memories washed over him, the horse continued across the muddy field, toward the back of the house. The field was higher than the yard, so he could see into it, could see that a tree had toppled over into the water pooled on the grass. Maybe the roots had turned up a mound of dirt, or maybe something else had made the hole. The pile was almost too neat, as if it had been shoveled there.

Maybe she'd thought the hole would drain away the water.

But as Forrest drew nearer, he peered into the hole and discovered it wasn't water filling it. Something else lay inside it, something all swaddled up in linen material smeared with mud and grime.

"What the hell…?" he murmured.

He swung his leg over the saddle and dismounted. His boot slipped on the muddy ground, but he used the horse to steady himself. Like all of the horses for the Cowboy Heroes, Mick was well trained and helpful. Forrest patted his mane in appreciation before stepping away from his mount and turning toward the hole. He leaned over and peered inside it, and his boot slipped again.

This time he didn't have the horse to steady himself, so his leg—his bad leg—went out from beneath him. As he began to fall, he reached out to catch himself. But like his boot, his fingers slipped on the mud, too, and he slid into the hole, knocking the loose dirt into it with him. It sprayed across that weird material.

Whatever it was, it had contoured to the shape of the object beneath it. But it wasn't an object.

It was a body with arms and legs and a face.

A mummy…like the one his brother Jonah had found. But unlike that body, Forrest suspected the storm hadn't turned up this one. Someone else had either dug it up or dug the hole to bury it here, like someone had buried the woman by the pharmaceutical company.

But why here? Why in Rae Lemmon's backyard?

Forrest reached into his pocket and pulled out his cell phone. He needed to call in a team to process the scene. Hopefully he could remove himself from it without compromising any evidence. After he called the coroner and some crime-scene techs, he shoved his phone back into his pocket and tried to pull himself out of the hole. Using his good leg, he dug his boot into the side of the hole and climbed out. As he pulled his boot free, some dirt tumbled down into the hole, next to the body, and the sun glinted off it.

It wasn't just dirt. There was something shiny beneath the mud and grime. Something metallic. Like coins or...

Buttons?

Had those belonged to the victim or the killer?

Rae closed her eyes and savored the silence. She would have to get up soon for work, but she had a few minutes to rest her eyes and relax. And after Connor had spent most of the night crying inconsolably, she needed some peace. He'd finally fallen back to sleep.

The pediatrician suspected the baby had colic, for which Rae blamed herself. The stress of law school, her job and single parenthood had affected her ability to produce breast milk and she now had to supplement with formula. When she'd called the doctor's service last night, she'd been told to switch to a soy-based formula, which she would do today on her way to bring Connor to day care.

Exhaustion gripped her, pulling her into oblivion. But she had been asleep for only a moment when a noise startled her. It wasn't the light *beep* of the alarm, but a loud pounding at a door. Worried that the knocking would wake up Connor, she rushed out of her bedroom without bothering to grab a robe. The only people who visited her were Bellamy and Maggie. Maybe Bellamy was back.

But she probably would have just let herself in; she had a copy and knew where the spare key was hidden. Disoriented for a moment from lack of sleep, Rae rushed to her front door and opened it. But nobody stood on her porch. If someone was there, they probably would have rung the bell.

The back door rattled as that fist pounded again. And a soft cry drifted from the nursery. Connor wasn't fully awake, but he was waking up. She ran across the living room and kitchen to pull open the door. "Shh," she cautioned her visitor. Then she gasped when she recognized the man standing before her. "What—what are you doing here?"

What the hell was he doing there? Especially now?

She had to look like death—after her sleepless night—with dark circles beneath her eyes, and her hair standing on end. And her nightgown...

She glanced down at the oversize T-shirt an old boyfriend had left behind. At least she'd gotten something comfy out of the relationship. But she hadn't expected much. Her experience with her father had taught her to never count on a man to stick around, and every boyfriend she'd ever had had reinforced that lesson.

That was why she'd chosen to be a single mother. She didn't need a husband to have a family. She didn't need a man. But this one…

He was so damn good-looking, even with mud on his clothes and smeared across his cheek. A fission of concern passed through her. "Did you get thrown?" she asked. Over his shoulder—his very broad shoulder—she caught a glimpse of a dark horse pawing at the muddy grass. "Are you okay?"

"I did not get thrown," he said, his voice sharp as if she'd stung his pride.

Or maybe that was just the way he always talked. He'd sounded that way when he'd told her that she couldn't be serious about asking him to dance.

Her face heated with embarrassment, but she didn't know if it was because of what had happened then or how unkempt she looked now. And with the way he kept staring at her, he couldn't have missed it. He was probably horrified.

"Then what are you doing here?" she asked again.

"I've called the police."

"I thought you were the police," she said. She knew, from the news reports and the gossip around Whisperwood, that the chief and his brothers had successfully talked him into investigating the murders.

"I am," he said. "That's why I called. I need to tape off your backyard. It's a crime scene."

Despite the heat of the August day, a cold chill raced down her spine and raised goose bumps on her skin. "Crime scene?" she asked. "What are you talking about?"

"I found something in your yard," he said.

"Why were you searching my property?" she asked. "Did you have a warrant?"

His face flushed now.

"I know my rights," she said. "If you didn't have a warrant, your search was illegal."

"I was surveying the flood damage," he said, "and your yard was in plain view from the field behind it."

Which was his family's property. In Whisperwood, the Coltons' ranch was second in size only to the Corgan spread.

"So you weren't even acting as a lawman when you performed this illegal search?" she asked. "You were just riding around your own property?"

His brow furrowed, and he opened his mouth to answer her, but she cut him off with a, "How dare you!"

She'd thought she'd let it go—her embarrassment over how he'd rejected her request to dance. But now that embarrassment turned to anger, which she unleashed on him.

Or maybe her exhaustion had made her extra irritable.

"You're trespassing on my property," she continued. "And when your fellow officers arrive, they will be obligated to issue you a citation."

"Rae—"

"You're not above the law," she said, "just because you're a Colton."

"I know I'm not above the law," he said, his face

still flushed, but with anger now. It burned in his hazel eyes, as well. "And neither are you."

"I am a law student," she said. "And I'm already working as a paralegal. I probably know the law better than you do."

He snorted then. "I've been a police officer for years," he reminded her. "I know the law. Why did *you* switch from managing the general store to law?"

She narrowed her eyes and studied his handsome face. He'd barely talked to her at her friend and his brother's wedding, so why was he curious about her now? Especially since he seemed to know more about her than she'd realized.

She was proud of her decision to go to law school, so she answered him, "I want to do something about all the crimes happening around Whisperwood."

"Then you should want me to investigate what I found on your property," he pointed out.

Now she was curious, which she probably would have been right way if she wasn't so damn exhausted. "What did you find?" she asked.

"A body."

She gasped in shock and shook her head. "No." It wasn't possible. Someone couldn't have been murdered in her backyard, where she'd imagined her son playing as he grew up, just like she had played there as a child. She shuddered and murmured again, "No."

Forrest nodded. "I'm afraid it's true."

"But—but I didn't hear anything." Wouldn't she have heard something if someone had been murdered in her backyard? But with work and school, she was gone so much that she probably hadn't even been home when it had happened. "I didn't see anything amiss."

"Have you missed anyone?" he asked. "Somebody staying with you that suddenly disappeared?"

She shook her head. Somebody had disappeared years ago on Rae, but that had been his choice to leave. Nobody had murdered him, although she'd sometimes wished she would have…when she'd watched her mother suffer.

"So you didn't notice anything in the backyard? Any digging?" he asked, persisting with his questions.

She shook her head again. "Why the hell would someone bury a body in my backyard?"

"I'm not sure if they'd just buried it, or if it was just uncovered," Forrest said. "It could have been there awhile."

"Like the body that Maggie and Jonah found after the hurricane?" she asked.

They had just stumbled across the body—the mummified body. She shivered with revulsion. What if that was what Forrest had found in her backyard? Another mummy?

"I'll know more once the coroner arrives," he continued.

The wail of a siren grew louder as it came closer to her house. Maybe the coroner was arriving now, along with the squad cars with the flashing lights that were pulling into her driveway.

Connor cried out now, and it wasn't a sleepy little cry but a wail almost as loud as the siren.

"What the hell is that?" Forrest asked in alarm.

And Rae bristled all over again with outrage. "*That* is my son," she replied as she hurried off to the nursery.

Tension gripped the chief, and he tightened his grasp on his cell phone before sliding it back into his pocket.

Behind him, sitting on the porch of his two-story farmhouse, Hays Colton chuckled. "Forrest has always had good timing," he said of his son. "You drive out here, looking for him, and he calls you like he somehow knew."

Chief Thompson shook his head. "That's not why he called." And he could have pointed out that Forrest's timing wasn't always perfect, or young Colton wouldn't have taken that bullet in his leg. But if his instincts weren't as strong as they were, he might have taken that bullet in his heart or his head instead of his leg.

He had survived.

His shooter had not.

"What's wrong?" Hays asked, his blue eyes wide with alarm. "Is he all right?"

Thompson nodded. "Yeah, he just called to give me a heads-up."

"Did he find out the identity of that poor girl found at the pharmaceutical company?"

The chief shook his head. "I wish that was why he called. Or better yet, to tell me he caught the killer." Because it would probably hit the news soon anyway, Archer Thompson shared, "He found another body."

Another person for the already overworked coroner to identify.

"I'm sorry," Hays said. He rose from the porch

swing, set his coffee cup on the railing and reached out to pat Thompson's shoulder.

They'd known each other for a long time, but Thompson didn't need any more sympathy. He needed answers—about his sister's murder and about these bodies that had recently turned up. He uttered a ragged sigh as he pushed himself up from the rocking chair in which he'd been sitting. He didn't move as fast as he once had, his bones aching now with age and over-use. He didn't stand quite as straight and tall as he once had either.

Neither did Hays, though, who had spent too many of his seventy-some years in the saddle, working his ranch. "My son will find out who really killed your sister," Hays assured him.

Thompson wanted to believe the killer was Elliot Corgan, because then he would have the satisfaction of knowing the sick bastard had died in prison. But Elliot had denied killing his sister, and there was no way he could have killed that woman whose body had been discovered in the Lone Star Pharma parking lot.

There was another killer in Whisperwood.

And until he was caught, the chief had a feeling that bodies would keep turning up.

Chapter 3

Cries emanated from the house, drawing Forrest's attention back to the one-story ranch structure and to *her*. A shadow passed behind the windows as if she was pacing in her kitchen. She had a baby.

Somebody had probably mentioned it to Forrest, but he didn't remember. He'd been preoccupied with the hurricane damage and now with the murder investigation. He surveyed the crime scene. Techs worked on bagging those corroded coins or buttons he'd uncovered, while the coroner worked on removing the body from the hole. They knew what they were doing; they didn't need his supervising their every move. In fact they'd probably resent it if he did.

So he headed back to the house. He raised his fist to the frame around the glass in the back door but hesitated before knocking. The cries were louder now, so he wasn't at risk of waking the baby.

The little guy was already awake and squalling. Seeing through the glass that Rae had her hands full with the baby, Forrest reached instead for the knob, turned it and let himself back into the house.

She gasped at his bold intrusion, but then she didn't seem to like anything he did. The invitation to dance had definitely been extended out of obligation or pity. Probably obligation…because she didn't seem to like him enough to pity him.

She glared at him over the baby's head. "Why did they have to come here with the sirens blaring?" she asked. "It doesn't look like an emergency."

"No," he agreed. The body was far beyond help. Rae Lemmon looked as if she needed help, though, as she rocked the baby's stiff little body in her arms.

Dark circles rimmed her brown eyes, but instead of detracting from her beauty, they highlighted it. She looked both vulnerable with her delicate features and sexy as hell with the old T-shirt molded to her generous curves.

"He had just finally gone to sleep," she murmured with a little catch in her voice, "when the sirens woke him up."

A pang of regret struck Forrest. The officers hadn't needed to put on the sirens. It would have been better to draw less attention to the scene than more.

Fortunately no reporters had followed them. Forrest had never enjoyed dealing with the press. So he definitely should have advised the police not to use the sirens when he'd called in what he'd found. He opened his mouth to apologize, but before he could, chimes rang out.

Was that the sound of her doorbell?

Maybe a reporter had picked up on the call after all. He grimaced—just as Rae held out the baby toward him.

"That's my phone," she said, as she handed him the crying infant.

Because he had no experience with babies, he didn't know how to hold him. But he reacted instinctively, closing his hands around the baby's midsection. Was he supposed to cup his head or something? He moved one hand to the baby's neck, and the little guy's head swiveled toward him.

The face that had been scrunched up with cries froze with shock, and his dark eyes widened as he stared up at Forrest. Was he scared?

His crying stopped, though, so that was a good thing. Forrest could hear himself think again. He could also hear the soft murmur of Rae's voice as she spoke to someone—maybe the baby's father. She must have left the phone in another room, since in order to answer it she'd left him alone with her baby.

Forrest was as frozen with fear as the little guy was. What if he was holding him wrong? Or he dropped him?

Rae would hate him even more then.

And Forrest would hate himself. But the kid was light and easy to hold. Maybe he could do this. And if he figured it out, he would actually be able to hold

Donovan and Bellamy's baby once it came, and not harm his little niece and nephew.

He crooked his arm and eased the baby into that, so the kid could stare up at him more comfortably. And he kept staring like he had no idea what the hell Forrest was, let alone whom. Keeping his deep voice to a low rumble, he murmured, "I'm Detective Colton."

Not that the baby could actually understand him. But he stared up at Forrest's face as if he was listening.

Maybe Forrest reminded him of his father. Where was the guy? Forrest didn't remember seeing anyone hanging around Rae at the wedding. But then, as one of the maids of honor, she'd been busy. Not too busy to ask him to dance, though.

But that must have been just part of her duty as a maid of honor—to look after the guests. Maybe that was why the baby's father had made himself scarce. Or maybe he'd stayed home to watch the baby, since he probably would have been newly born at the time of the wedding.

She hadn't looked like she'd recently given birth then, though—not with how well her navy blue maid of honor's dress had fit her.

Forrest had so many questions about Rae Lemmon, so much curiosity. It was that curiosity that had drawn him to her house this morning and to the body in her backyard. That—more than anything—should have proved to him that she was going to be trouble.

He had to restrict his curiosity to professional only, since his broken engagement had convinced him that personal relationships were not for him. The only personal relationships he was going to allow himself was with his family.

Being around this little guy might help him prepare for the new baby so that he would be able to help Donovan and Bellamy when they needed it. So that he could be a good uncle to the little cowgirl or cowboy that the newlyweds would have.

"What about you?" Forrest asked the baby. "Are you going to be a cowboy? You want to learn to ride?"

Despite having no experience with kids, he realized this one was too young to answer any of his questions, but the baby seemed fascinated by his voice. Those already wide brown eyes widened even more. With those enormous eyes, delicate features and brown hair, the baby looked so much like his beautiful mother.

A little bubble floated out of the baby's lips as he gurgled. And Forrest tensed with concern. Was something wrong?

And where had the baby's mother gone?

Forrest had felt more comfortable finding that mummified body in her backyard than he did standing in her kitchen, holding her child. That body was beyond saving; the only thing he needed to do for her was find her killer.

But the baby…

He could screw up. He could cause him harm, and that was the last thing he wanted to do.

Why had the crying stopped?

What had Forrest Colton done to her baby?

Rae peered through her open bedroom door at the

man standing in her kitchen. He'd moved Connor to the crook of his muscular arm, and her child lay there, staring up in adulation at the man holding him.

Connor hadn't looked at her that way in a while—with fascination. Frustration, instead, scrunched up his little face when he stared up at her. He'd been so fussy lately.

For her.

But not for Forrest Colton.

What the hell had the man done to him?

"Rae? Are you there? Are you okay?"

It wasn't his deep voice rumbling in her ear as she pressed the cell phone into the crook of her shoulder and tried to dress while peering through the crack of her door. "Yes, Kenneth, I'm fine," she assured her caller, who was one of the lawyers at the firm where she worked as a paralegal.

"Do you need me to come out there?"

"No," she automatically replied. She'd been saying that to him a lot since she'd been hired at the firm—no to an offer of coffee or dinner. Not that he was harassing her. He'd made it clear that he was happily married and that his offers were only intended to make her feel welcome at the firm.

"I just wanted to be available in case any legal issues arise out of this search of your property," he explained. "You're one of the family here at Lukas, Jolley and Fitzsimmons." He was more family than she was because he was related by marriage. His father-in-law was Fitzsimmons.

"I'm actually going to leave soon." Even though this

was her home, she didn't want to stay here while Forrest Colton was on her property. "I'll drop off Connor at day care and come into the office."

Kenneth blew out a ragged breath of relief. "That'll be good for you to get out of there."

He'd called because he'd heard on his police scanner that the coroner and a crime-scene unit had been dispatched to her address. He used the scanner to drum up business for the firm—chasing ambulances.

"Yes," she agreed. It would be good for her to get away from Forrest Colton. And to get him away from her child. "I'll see you soon," she said as she clicked off her cell phone.

While juggling the phone, she'd managed to replace her nightgown with a long summer dress. She'd even managed to rub some concealer over her dark circles and cover it up with a dusting of powder. A swipe of mascara across her lashes finished her makeup routine.

She stepped out of the bedroom and rushed into the kitchen. Forrest looked up from her son and focused on her face.

Did he notice the makeup? Did he think she'd put it on for him?

The heat of embarrassment rushed up now, probably flushing her face under that thin dusting of powder. "I had to take that call," she told him.

"Was it your husband?" he asked.

A chortle slipped through her lips at the thought of her being married. "Not mine," she said.

"Somebody else's?" he asked.

She grimaced. "Don't make it sound like *that*. He's

one of my colleagues. He heard the call and was concerned."

Forrest's brow furrowed. "How did he hear it?"

She shrugged. It wasn't illegal to own a police scanner, but since starting law school, she'd already grown tired of the ambulance-chaser comments.

"What about you?" he asked. "Did you hear anything last night?"

"I already told you I hadn't," she reminded him. Then she pointed toward the baby, who'd actually fallen asleep now in Forrest's arms. "He's the only one who's been making any noise around here at night."

The detective looked down at the baby again, and his lips curved into a smile, which was quite a turnaround from the grimace of horror that had crossed his face when she had first handed him her son. "What's his name?" he asked.

"Connor."

He glanced up at her as if waiting for more.

So she added, "Lemmon."

"You're not married?" he asked.

"I thought I already established that," she said. When she'd asked him to dance at that wedding.

She was old-fashioned enough that she wouldn't have asked a single guy to dance if she was married. But apparently she wasn't as old-fashioned as he was.

"You know you don't have to be married to have a baby," she said.

"The father didn't want to marry you?"

Both outraged and offended, she gasped. Forrest

Colton wasn't just old-fashioned; he was a jerk. "The father doesn't even know me."

He gasped now.

And she laughed at the shock on his face.

Her son tensed briefly in Forrest's arm, but he moved him in a rocking motion, and Connor settled back to sleep. How could the man soothe her son while he riled her up? She'd never met anyone who'd infuriated her as much as Forrest Colton did.

"I chose to have my son on my own," she informed him. "I used a sperm donor." And before he could jump to another unflattering assumption about her, she added, "From a sperm bank."

"Oh," he murmured.

Not everyone understood or appreciated what she'd done. But she didn't care. She loved Connor so much— even when he kept her awake. She moved closer to Forrest and brushed a fingertip along Connor's cheek. He was so perfect.

"You chose to be a single parent," he murmured.

And she couldn't tell if he approved or disapproved. But she didn't give a damn what he thought anyway.

"He's the only male I need or want in my life," she informed Forrest, just like she'd told her friends a week ago. She didn't want anyone to answer to, anyone to disappoint or abandon her.

"That's too bad," he said.

And she gasped with surprise yet again. Was he… interested in her after all? She glanced from Connor's face to his, which was flushed now.

"I meant…because it would be safer for you and

Connor if you weren't out here alone," he said quickly, as if he was worried she'd misunderstood him.

She sighed. "You sound like Bellamy and Maggie," she admitted.

"They're concerned about you, too?"

She nodded. And that had been before Forrest's discovery in her backyard. She couldn't imagine how much they would worry now. She was surprised that he was concerned, though.

Why?

He barely knew her. And if he was interested in her, he wouldn't act like such a jerk. Maybe it was just the lawman in him that had him worried about her safety.

"Your friends are wise to worry about you being out here all by yourself," he said.

"They're my friends, so they should know better than anyone else does that I can take care of myself and my son without the help or protection of any man," she informed him.

"I'm not saying you need a man," Forrest told her. "I'm saying that you need someone, though. You're training to be a lawyer, not a police officer."

She tensed. "You really believe I'm in danger?"

He shrugged, which jostled the sleeping baby into opening one eye and peering up at the man holding him.

If she was in danger, Connor would be, as well. So she had to ask, "What do you think?"

"I think there's a killer in Whisperwood," he said. "So nobody's safe."

She reached for her son, taking him from the detective's arm. When her fingers brushed across his muscular forearm, a tingling sensation rose from her fingertips to her heart, jolting her.

And Connor.

He awoke with a cry of protest. Apparently he'd preferred Forrest Colton holding him over his mother holding him. But then he had to be frustrated with her; she hadn't managed to comfort him last night, hadn't managed to make him feel better, like her mother had always made her feel better.

Even when Mama had been so very sick, she'd offered solace to Rae, had held her and soothed all of her fears. She missed her mom every day. And she needed her now more than she ever had.

Because Rae was scared...and not just of the killer on the loose. She was scared that she may have taken on more than she could handle alone.

She was alone.

He had watched the house all day, had watched the police collect their evidence, had watched Rae Lemmon leave and then return later, after the police had already gone for the day. So she was the only one near the house now.

She and her baby.

He waited outside, watching the house until all of the lights flickered off inside, leaving it dark. Then he moved away from the tree against which he'd been leaning, and he headed toward the house.

Beside the sidewalk leading up to the porch, a big iron pot overflowed with red geraniums that matched the flowers overflowing the window boxes of the little white ranch house. He bent over, tipped the pot and fumbled beneath it.

Then a grin curved his lips, and his fingers closed around a key and tugged it free from beneath the pot. A magnet glued to the key had kept it stuck to the bottom. With the key in hand, he climbed the short steps up to the porch. As he moved across it to the front door, boards creaked beneath his weight. He unlocked the door, and it creaked as he opened it.

He tensed, waiting for lights to flash on inside, but everything remained dark and quiet.

The house was small, just two bedrooms off the living room, with a bathroom in between them. The door to the first bedroom was mostly closed, so he walked past it and the bathroom to the second bedroom. Moonlight streaming through the window reflected off the glow-in-the-dark stars painted on the ceiling. That light shone down on the face of the baby sleeping in the crib.

He crossed the room to the crib and stared down at the sleeping child. Something twisted in his chest, and he sucked in a breath.

He hated to do this.

But he had no choice.

Not anymore.

His hand shaking, he pulled a switchblade from his pocket and popped out the blade. Then he leaned over the railing of the crib, with the knife in his hand extended toward the sleeping child…

Chapter 4

Chief Archer Thompson was in over his head. He knew it. That was why he'd hired the detective from Austin—Forrest Colton. He hadn't done that just because Hurricane Brooke had stretched the department so thin that it was nearly transparent. He'd hired Forrest because Archer was too close to one of the murder victims.

His hand shook as he reached for the picture on the bookshelf in his home study. Emmeline at sixteen. So beautiful...

So sweet.

The first body Hurricane Brooke had uncovered was his sister's. Missing for all of those years...

Was it the same situation with the body that Forrest had found out at the Lemmon house? Had her family been wondering for decades where she was?

And what about the woman in the parking lot?

She hadn't been dead long, but somebody was probably already missing her, wondering where she was, if she'd been hurt and stranded in the hurricane.

He didn't need the coroner's report to know that she'd been murdered like the others. Elliot Corgan was dead now, so he couldn't have hurt her.

And he claimed he hadn't hurt Emmeline.

But if not him, who? Who else would want to harm the sweet young woman his sister had been?

Yeah, he was in too deep—too emotionally invested in finding the killer. Forrest Colton wasn't. He would be able to examine everything with objectivity. He wouldn't have had all of the success he'd had solving those cold cases in Austin if he got too involved. So nothing and nobody should be able to distract Forrest from finding this killer.

He was distracted, so distracted with thoughts of Rae Lemmon and her sweet baby. Despite her insistence that she didn't need any protection, Forrest should have insisted on leaving an officer at her house. He could have convinced her that it was protocol—to protect the crime scene.

But it wasn't the crime scene he was worried about.

Her house was so far from town, so far from any other homestead. While some of his family's ranch touched her property, the closest other dwelling belonged to the Corgans. And one of them had been a serial killer. How the hell had Elliot Corgan's family kept the fact that he was a murderer out of the press for so many years?

Judicial order?

They must have paid the judge for that order. Had they paid for anything else in town? For someone else to start up the murders to try to make Elliot Corgan look innocent?

His blood chilled as the thought occurred to him. But why bother now after another Corgan had already been arrested? James Corgan had tried to kill his ex-wife, Maggie Reeves-Corgan, and Forrest's brother Jonah, who was now Maggie's fiancé. Fortunately James hadn't been as successful at committing murders as his great-uncle had.

Those old case files sat atop Forrest's desk, the top folders nearly sliding off the mound of records and onto the floor of his cubicle area of the Whisperwood Police Department. He'd looked through everything in those case files and was as convinced as the jury had been that Elliot had been responsible for all of those murders.

But one.

There had been one victim all those years ago that had been strangled but hadn't had a scarf stuffed in her mouth like the others. She'd also been the only one of those bodies that had been mummified.

Like the chief's sister…

Like the body found in Rae's backyard…

No. Even back then, before Elliot had been arrested, convicted and sentenced to life in prison, there had been two killers. Were there two killers now? Or had that one just started up again?

Had his first recent murder been Elliot's? After Jonah and Maggie had interviewed the serial killer in prison, he had supposedly committed suicide, but Jonah had had his doubts. And knowing serial killers as well he did, so did Forrest. Had this killer somehow gotten to Elliot to prevent the inmate from revealing *his* identity?

And if this killer could get to someone in a maximum-security prison, he could certainly get to someone who lived in a little ranch house outside town.

Forrest shivered despite the fact that the air conditioner barely worked in the big open area that was divided only by the short cubicle walls. Out of all of the cubicles, his was the only one currently occupied. The officers on duty had gone out on patrol hours ago. Except for the 911 area and the front desk, the building was pretty much deserted.

He needed to head home or his parents would worry. Despite all of the years he'd been gone or maybe because of them, his parents worried about him like he was a teenager staying out past curfew. Not that he ever stayed out late. It wasn't as if he had anyplace—but work—to go. And maybe that was why they worried.

He touched his bad leg, which was stiff from all of the time he'd been sitting at his desk. They were probably worried that he was going to get hurt again—like he'd been hurt before. Like he still was...

His leg shook, threatening to fold, but he locked it and walked stiff-legged around his desk. He'd just stepped outside the dingy fabric walls of his cubicle when the phone on his desk began to ring. Dispatch probably didn't realize he was still in the office, so the call hadn't come through them. It must have come into his direct line.

Dread gripped his stomach, churning it, as he hobbled back to his desk and picked up the receiver. "Detective Colton."

"This is Dr. Bentley from the medical examiner's office," the caller identified herself. "The ME wanted me to let you know that we're pretty certain of an identification for that murder victim."

Shocked, Forrest sucked in a breath. "That was quick."

"For the one in the parking lot," Dr. Bentley clarified. "Despite how well it was preserved, the other body may take a long time to identify."

The body in Rae's backyard.

His mind flitted to Rae Lemmon and to her son—to the two of them being alone in that house where the body had been buried just a few yards from their back door. And that dread gripped his stomach again.

He was more worried about her than he was about notifying the family of the murder victim from the parking lot. But he owed them his full attention; they'd already lost too much.

"Are you still at the office?" he asked the doctor.

"Yes, Detective."

"I'm going to come down and take a look at the full report," he said. Her family was going to want more than her identification; they were going to want to know what happened to her.

They were also going to want to know who did it to her. He couldn't give them that person's name. Not yet.

But he would. He had to stop this sadistic killer before he killed again. Before he hurt anyone else.

And again an image of Rae's pretty face flashed through his mind. She'd said she could take care of herself, so she was strong and resourceful. To get into law school, she also had to be smart. Too smart to take dangerous risks. He really had no reason to be worried about her.

But those other women had probably thought they could take care of themselves, too, that they needed no protection. Now they were lying in the morgue. He did not want Rae Lemmon to wind up there.

Despite how exhausted she was from all of her sleepless nights, Rae couldn't rest. Sleep continued to elude her. And it wasn't because Connor was crying.

He was quiet—so quiet that she felt goose bumps of unease lift her skin. Why was he so quiet now?

He was exhausted, too, though. Probably even more exhausted than she was, since he was the one who'd done all of the crying the past few nights. He must have just been sleeping soundly.

Like she wished she could sleep.

But unlike Connor, she wasn't blissfully unaware of what had been discovered in their backyard earlier that day. A body.

Whose?

Who had been killed, and had that murder taken place right here? In Rae's backyard? Or in her house?

She shivered at the thought.

Would Forrest come back? Would he want to bring his crime-scene techs into her home?

She'd left before they'd finished up in her backyard. But they'd been gone when she'd returned, leaving behind only that yellow tape that had cordoned off her backyard.

Not that she wanted to go out there ever again.

When she'd left, she'd locked up the house, so unless Forrest had found the key under the flowerpot, he wouldn't have been able to get inside without breaking and entering. And she'd found no evidence of that.

Unlike the backyard, her house had seemed undisturbed—or at the least just as messy as it had been when she and Connor had left. Would she have even been able to tell if Forrest had searched it?

Of course he must have realized he would need a warrant before she would allow that. She'd made it clear to him that she knew her rights and had no intention of letting him violate them or anything else.

But he'd violated her sleep. Thoughts of him—as much as thoughts of that poor corpse—had kept her awake. Why did he irritate her so much?

What was it about him that bothered her in a way she couldn't remember anyone else ever bothering her?

She turned to flip to her left side from her right, but the sheets twisted around her, prohibiting her from moving. A curse slipped out from between her lips.

And she tensed. Hopefully she hadn't awakened Connor. But she heard something else—a strange creaking noise, like something or someone moving across the floorboards.

Then Connor did awake with a cry. But this wasn't like the nights before, when colic had brought him out of an already fitful sleep. This sounded more like a cry of terror—but it might have held pain, as well.

Jerking at the tangled sheets, Rae fought her way out of the bed. Tripping and stumbling over the ends of the sheets, she picked herself up from the floor and ran from her bedroom into Connor's. If she'd met anyone between her door and his, she would have plowed them over; she was so desperate to get to her son.

But nobody crossed her path. And nobody stood inside the nursery, but there was something, some lingering presence, some scent…

And she knew that Connor had not been alone the entire night. Somebody had been in his room. She scrambled toward the crib and peered over the railing.

Connor's feet and arms flailed as he lay on his back, kicking and screaming. She reached down and picked him up, checking his tiny body for wounds or whatever was hurting him as she did.

He was stiff, but nothing felt wounded. She soothed him by rubbing her hand up and down his back, which was damp with perspiration from his exertion, and a few hairs stuck to her palm. Had he been thrashing so violently that he'd pulled out some hair?

Maybe she needed to call a doctor. Or take him to the emergency room.

She held him tightly against her and murmured soothing words as she continued to stroke his back and rock him. Her heart pounded frantically, and his smaller heart echoed that beat…until finally it slowed. And his terrified sobbing quieted to soft, shaky cries.

And with his crying no longer ringing in her ears, she could hear other things. Like that creak again…

But it wasn't a floorboard this time. It was the creak of a door opening, then the distinctive click of it closing again. She shuddered. Somebody had been inside the house, inside the nursery…with Connor.

She needed to call the police.

She'd been so anxious to get to Connor that she'd left her cell in her bedroom. Had the intruder been in there? Had he taken her phone? Her purse?

She didn't care if he'd taken everything she owned— as long as he didn't harm her son. Or her.

She had to make sure he didn't return. With Connor still clasped in her arms, she rushed out of his room and back to hers. Her fingers trembling, she flipped on the switch next to the door and illuminated the room with the ceiling light.

Her phone lay on the bedside table, connected to her charger, so she rushed over to it. But as she reached for it, she noticed something fluttering on her pillow in the breeze that blew in through the open window. A piece of paper.

But it wasn't just paper.

When she picked it up, short strands of brown hair rained out of it, onto her tangled sheets. She touched the strands, which were baby soft, and panic gripped her heart.

It was Connor's hair. She inspected his little head

and found where the piece had been cut, just above his left ear. But it looked like only his hair had been cut, the ends left jagged.

No blood smeared his pink skin.

He hadn't been hurt. But he could have been.

Or he could have been taken from her.

Someone had been inside her house. Inside the nursery and close enough to Connor to cut a lock of his hair.

She shivered with fear and revulsion.

Her poor baby…

Why? Why would someone have broken in to…?

What?

Remembering the note, she held it up to read the words crudely scrawled across the lined paper. *Get rid of the cop, or you'll lose your kid. For good.*

Get rid of the cop?

Forrest?

Or all of the police who'd been working the crime scene in her backyard?

That wasn't her fault. She hadn't found the body. She hadn't called them.

She glanced down at her phone. She couldn't call now for help. Whoever had left that note, whoever had been inside her house, might be outside—waiting, watching…

Seeing if she would ignore his warning.

And what would happen if she did?

Would he break back into her house? Would he come inside and steal Connor?

Or kill him?

Chapter 5

She had a name now. The body found during the parking-lot excavation belonged to twenty-year-old Patrice Eccleston. Patrice's family had reported her missing shortly after Hurricane Brooke had struck the Gulf Coast.

They weren't sure when they'd talked to her last, though, and couldn't pinpoint an exact moment when she had disappeared. Nobody knew what she would have been doing anywhere near Lone Star Pharma.

Forrest had come back to the crime scene. He needed to release it so that the construction could continue on the parking-lot extension. But first he needed to make sure nothing had been missed—nothing that might lead them to Patrice's killer.

Her body had been found late in the afternoon, so

the scene had been processed into the night. Something could have been missed.

Not bandages and embalming fluid, though. She hadn't been mummified like the other bodies. But he wondered... Was that because the killer had been interrupted? Or because he was too old to handle the bodies as he once had?

It would have taken strength to strangle Patrice. She was young and very fit. She would have been strong, too. She would have fought.

The coroner had confirmed signs of a struggle in the bruises and scratches. Poor Patrice had fought for her life. But she'd lost.

Forrest needed to find who had won. Who had taken the young woman's life way too soon?

The yellow tape sagged between the thin metal posts that had been planted between the mounds of dirt and the backhoe that had dug up those mounds and the body. The body of Patrice Eccleston.

Why here?

And why her?

Had she known the person who'd murdered her? Or had a stranger chosen her at random?

So many questions...

But even though he now had her name, Forrest still had no answers to those questions. To the ones that would give Patrice's grieving family true comfort.

Forrest lifted his stiff leg and stepped over the sagging tape, his boot sinking deep into the soft earth on the other side. The freshly dug up soil reminded him of the crime scene at Rae Lemmon's house. Hurricane Brooke hadn't brought up that body like she had the corpse of the chief's long-missing younger sister. Someone else had brought up that body, had dug it up just like this one had been dug up.

But Patrice had been inadvertently dug up during the parking-lot extension. The body in Rae's backyard had appeared to have been intentionally dug up.

What the hell was going on?

Forrest walked around the crime scene, moving closer to the hole where Patrice's body had been. Had something been missed? Was there a clue here like those old coins or buttons or whatever he'd discovered at Rae's?

He pulled out one of the posts holding up the sagging tape and began to poke through the mounds of dirt. A soft metallic clink rang out as his makeshift tool struck something within the dirt. Using the pole as a shovel, he moved the soil aside until he uncovered a trio of coins. Or buttons.

Leaning over, he peered closer to inspect them. These were caked with dirt and grime like the ones he'd found in Rae Lemmon's backyard. Exactly like the ones he'd found in Rae's backyard despite this being a recent crime scene and that an old one.

Or was it?

Had the body just been moved there?

He needed to find out why these scenes were linked. And how Rae Lemmon's property and Rae figured into these murders if at all.

Despite locking all of the windows and barricading the front door, Rae hadn't been able to fall back to sleep the night before. She'd felt *him* out there.

She didn't know who *he* was, but she'd had no doubt that he was somewhere close enough to watch her, to see what she would do. If she would disregard his warning.

She'd wanted to so badly. She'd wanted to call the police. Or at least her friends.

But her friends would have insisted that she call the police or, worse yet, Forrest Colton. And she hadn't been willing to risk it—to risk her son's life—for anything.

Maybe she would have fallen back to sleep if she hadn't stayed in his room, curled up in the chair next to his crib. Despite his late-night haircut, Connor had had no issues falling back to sleep. Maybe what had happened had seemed just like a bad dream to him.

Rae wished that it had been. But the note and that little clipped lock of hair proved that it hadn't been just a nightmare. It had happened.

It could not happen again. No stranger could get that close to her son.

An image flitted through her mind—an image of Forrest Colton holding Connor so easily and comfortably in the crook of his strong arm. The baby had been so content after such a fussy night. Connor obviously hadn't felt as if Forrest was a stranger.

But he would have to be one now. He would have to stay away from her and her child.

While Connor had slept in, she'd showered and dressed for work—not that she had any urge to go. But as a single mom, she was the only one who could pay the bills—for day care, for food, for utilities...

She didn't have to pay for the house. Her mother had

left it to her when she'd passed away last year. Mama had bought the house before she'd met Rae's father, and she'd always refused to put him on the deed. She'd probably worried that if she had, he would have lost it somehow. Instead she'd lost her husband. When she'd gotten sick, he'd just taken off.

That had proved to Rae that men couldn't be trusted, and she vowed to never need anyone. Which was good because none of the guys she'd dated had chosen to stick around either.

She leaned over the crib railing and brushed her finger across Connor's cheek. But she needed this little guy. Even though he'd been in her life only for a short time, she couldn't imagine her life without him.

And she vowed now that she would never have to because she would make damn certain that nothing happened to him.

An engine rumbled outside the closed window as a vehicle pulled up to the house. Why hadn't she heard that last night? Had the intruder arrived on foot? Or horseback as Forrest had the morning before?

Connor must have heard the engine, too, because he opened his eyes and stared sleepily up at her. Had he seen the person last night? He must have, because he'd cried out with such fear. He'd seen whoever had broken into their home. If only he could talk.

She picked him up from the crib and clasped him close to her before walking through the house to peer out at the driveway. And a curse slipped out of her lips when she spied the police SUV and the man who stepped out of it.

Forrest Colton.

She glanced around the SUV, around the driveway and front yard. But she couldn't see anyone lurking out there now. Maybe he'd gone with the dawn, since he'd had no shadows left to hide in. Or maybe he was still there.

Still watching her.

And now he would see that Forrest was here despite his warning. He would think that she had ignored it.

That she didn't care.

Fear gripping her, Rae clasped Connor so tightly that he tensed and began to cry. If not for his crying, she would have pretended that they weren't home. But Forrest knew they were, and he rang the bell.

Keeping Connor against her with just one arm holding him now, she used her other hand to jerk the chair from beneath the door handle. Not that she intended to let Forrest in.

She opened the door but stood inside the jamb and coldly asked him, "What do you want?"

His brow furrowed for a moment with confusion and then he glanced at Connor, who continued to cry. "Oh, did he keep you awake last night, too?"

Too? Did he know about the intruder?

Then she remembered that he knew about her sleepless night before he'd discovered that body in her backyard. "No, not him."

He raised a brow, as if silently asking who.

But she wasn't about to tell him about the reason she really hadn't slept. So she just shook her head and reminded him, "It's none of your business."

"Actually, it is," he said. "Your property is a crime scene. I need to know who's had access to it. Who has been visiting you?"

She wished she knew. "My friends come by—you know them, Maggie and Bellamy."

That eyebrow arched again. "Nobody else?"

"I don't know," she answered honestly. "I haven't seen anyone else."

But she knew someone had been there. She had proof of it—not that she was going to show it to Forrest. No. She had to get rid of Forrest as soon as possible. So she began to close the door. "If that's all, I really need to get ready for work."

Somehow his foot had crossed the threshold, and his leg pressed against the door, stopping her from closing it on him. "You look dressed," he murmured gruffly, and something like disappointment flashed through his hazel eyes.

He couldn't have actually found her sleep shirt sexy, though. Or her.

She wore black dress pants now with a blouse buttoned all the way to her neck. The partners at the law firm were very conservative—even Kenneth Dawson, despite his ambulance-chasing tendencies.

"I need to get Connor ready to bring to day care," she said.

His cries had quieted, but he squirmed against her. Awake now, he had to be hungry. Fortunately he felt dry or she might have had to change herself again with as closely as she'd been holding him.

Forrest's eyes narrowed now as he stared at her. "Is something wrong?" he asked.

Heat climbed to her face, but she shook her head. "No. I'm just busy—so busy that I don't have time to keep telling you that I don't have any information to help you. I don't know anything about how that body wound up in the backyard. I can't help you!" She put her shoulder behind the door now, trying to squeeze Forrest out.

"You need help," he said.

And she froze. What did he know?

"Don't go getting all defensive," he said. "I know you think you can handle everything all by yourself."

She did get defensive now, as her pride smarted from his remark. "I can."

He pointed toward the chair next to the door. "You're obviously scared."

"A body was found in my backyard," she reminded him.

"You weren't scared yesterday," he said.

"I didn't have time to think about it," she admitted. Or she would have realized that he was right—that she was in danger and vulnerable out here on her own.

"Think about reaching out for help," he advised her.

She shook her head. "I don't need or want your help!"

"I wasn't volunteering," he said. "I was thinking about your friends, Maggie and Bellamy."

Her face got hotter with embarrassment. Of course she should have realized that he wasn't offering his personal protection or help. He hadn't even wanted to dance with her. If she told him about what had happened the night before, about the warning, he would probably assign another officer to her case. He had bigger cases to solve than finding out who had threatened her.

"Bellamy is on her honeym—"

"She and Donovan get back today," he interrupted. "And Maggie hasn't gone anywh—"

"Without Jonah," she said. And while he wasn't actually a police officer, he was one of the Cowboy Heroes, and maybe her intruder considered him law enforcement, as well.

"Don't you like my brother?" Forrest asked, and he seemed defensive now.

She sighed. "I like Jonah. I especially like how happy he makes Maggie. I don't want to intrude on their new relationship." That was very true. She was so happy for her friend that she didn't want to dump her worries on her, especially after everything Maggie had just been through with her crazy ex-husband.

"I know my brothers wouldn't consider your reaching out to your friends to be an intrusion," he said. "And while I don't know Bellamy and Maggie that well yet, I doubt they would be your friends if *they* considered your asking for help an intrusion."

"They wouldn't," she admitted. Hell, they would be happy to help if she reached out. Too happy.

And once they knew what had happened last night, they would insist that she report it to the police and probably to Forrest in particular, since his investigation in her backyard must have been what had precipitated the threat.

Why?

She wanted to know who had been buried back there. More important she wanted to know who had done it and for that person to be brought to justice. But she wasn't willing to risk her baby's life for it or for anyone.

"I need to get to work," she said as she leaned against the door again, trying to push it closed—on Forrest. "So you need to leave." Before anyone saw him here. "Now!" Her voice cracked with desperation.

He kept his boot planted on her threshold, and his body planted in the doorway, and he was too big, too muscular, for her to move. His hazel eyes narrowed again, and he leaned closer to study her face.

She sucked in a breath as an intense feeling gripped her. It wasn't fear this time. It was...

The same thing she'd felt when she'd asked him to dance at the wedding. Sure, she'd felt sorry for how alone he'd seemed that night. But that wasn't the only reason why she'd asked him to dance. She'd been attracted to him. Then. And now.

Forrest Colton was so damn good-looking, so sexy...

But she couldn't give in to that attraction—even as he leaned closer, so close that his lips could have brushed across hers. If she rose on tiptoe, if she lifted her mouth.

Temptation tugged at her. But the last thing she wanted the intruder to see was her kissing Forrest

Colton…even if she wanted so badly to do it, so badly that a cry of frustration slipped out between her lips.

"Please," she murmured. "Please leave me alone."

As if she'd slapped him, he jerked his head up and stepped back. And finally she was able to slam the door between them. She slammed it with such force that Connor began to scream.

Regret gripped her now as powerfully as that attraction had. And she wasn't just regretful that she'd upset her son. She regretted not kissing Forrest Colton. But maybe he hadn't intended to kiss her at all.

Maybe she'd just imagined his intent, just like she wished she'd imagined that man breaking into her home the night before. When she left the house moments later to leave for work, Forrest was still parked in her driveway. And there was no trace of attraction on his face, just irritation…with her.

"Why are you still here?" she asked.

He held up a piece of paper. "I got that warrant you told me I needed," he said.

Her brow furrowed. "Warrant? But you already searched my property without it."

"Not the house," he said.

"You want to search the house?" She tensed.

He nodded. "And this piece of paper gives me the legal authority to conduct that search."

She only glanced at the paper, which must have been printed from one those mini printers officers used to issue citations in their vehicles. Then she shrugged. "Whatever. You won't find anything." She stepped back onto the porch and unlocked the door for him.

He wouldn't find the note. She'd tucked that into her purse, sealed in a plastic bag, along with that lock of hair. "Just lock up when you leave."

As if that mattered.

The intruder had gotten in easily enough last night that she hadn't even heard him until Connor had cried out. Was he out there now?

Watching?

And what would he do about Forrest's being here again? Over his staying to search the house?

Would he make good on his threat?

Tears rushed to her eyes, and she blinked furiously as she turned away. But Forrest must have seen them, because he caught her arm, the one from which Connor's car carrier swung. He turned her back toward him.

"Are you okay?" he asked, his deep voice sounding even deeper with concern.

She closed her eyes and willed the tears away. "I…" She couldn't tell him.

As if he'd read her mind, he implored her, "You can tell me."

But she shook her head. "I have to go." She jerked away from him and rushed toward her small SUV. Hopefully her intruder had seen that and realized that she was doing everything she could to get rid of Forrest.

Unless…

Unless he didn't just want the detective to go away. Maybe he wanted him dead.

Chapter 6

She had been on his mind since she'd left him alone that morning to search her house. Hell, she'd been on his mind even before that, even before he'd found that body in her backyard. She'd been on his mind since he'd seen her, looking so damn beautiful, at Donovan and Bellamy's wedding.

Maybe that was why he was here. Not just to welcome the newlyweds back but to get insight into the woman who confused and fascinated and aggravated Forrest.

He'd nearly kissed her that morning. His skin heated and his pulse quickened just thinking about it, about how close his mouth had come to hers—so close that he'd nearly tasted her minty breath.

He wished he'd tasted her mouth, wished that he'd

given in to temptation and kissed her, even though he knew that would have been wrong. Or at the very least unprofessional.

Not that he considered her a murder suspect. But he had found a body in her backyard. And he had a feeling she knew more than she was admitting, that there was something she was keeping from him. And that was why she seemed so damn scared.

Not that she didn't have reason to be, though. There was a killer on the loose in Whisperwood.

Forrest had to find him.

"I guess we bored him into a stupor," Bellamy remarked with a giggle.

Donovan snorted. "Forrest usually gets like this when he's working a case, so single-minded that solving it is all he can think about."

He did get that way—until now, until this case. Now he kept thinking about Rae Lemmon instead of the case. His mind was totally focused on her. And how the hell was he going to catch a killer like that?

Unless she knew who the killer was. Was that why she'd been so anxious to get rid of him that morning? Was she trying to protect someone?

"And he's not working one case but two." Donovan continued to talk about Forrest as if he wasn't even there.

"Two?" Bellamy asked and then nodded. "You mean the chief's sister and the body found in the parking lot. Of course with so many years between the deaths, it's unlikely the murders would be related."

Forrest wasn't so sure about that, but he wasn't about

to share his suspicions with Bellamy when she obviously didn't have all of the facts yet. They had just returned from their honeymoon and were currently in the kitchen of Bellamy's house, unpacking groceries they must have just picked up from the store.

Forrest had called Donovan and informed him of the body he'd found in Rae's backyard, but obviously he hadn't shared that news with his bride yet. And apparently she hadn't learned about the body from anyone else either.

Like Rae.

Why was she so damn stubbornly independent that she refused to reach out even to her friends? Why was she so determined to do everything on her own?

"What?" Bellamy asked as she looked from him to Donovan and back. "Has something else happened?"

"I didn't want to upset you," Donovan began, "especially now."

"I'm pregnant," Bellamy said, "not fragile. I can handle getting upset, which is lucky for you since I'm getting pretty upset right now."

"Uh, maybe I should go," Forrest murmured as he started to rise from the chair he'd taken at the kitchen table.

But Bellamy shoved him back into his seat. "What's going on?" she asked him.

He looked to his brother, who just nodded at him. "I found another body."

She shuddered. "Oh, no."

That wasn't the worst part of it, and she needed to know, so he added, "In Rae's backyard."

She turned back to her husband. "And you didn't tell me?"

Not wanting any trouble between the newlyweds, Forrest jumped in to explain, "It just happened yesterday."

"You weren't feeling well," Donovan reminded her.

"I was tired," she said. Then she touched her belly, which had swelled. She was showing now. "We were tired."

Donovan slipped his arm around her and kissed her forehead. "I was going to tell you but then this guy showed up." His brother focused on him again. "Why did you show up? I'm not thinking that it was just to welcome us back and hear about the amazing time we had."

"I did want to make sure you had a good time," Forrest said. His brother and Bellamy certainly deserved their happiness.

"But…" Donovan prodded him. "What else?"

Forrest turned toward his new sister-in-law again. "I wanted to ask you about Rae."

"She's my best friend."

"So there's no one who knows her better?"

She shook her head. "We grew up together. We've been friends since kindergarten. But I think we grew up even more later in life, when we had to deal with ailing parents. Rae's dad took off when her mom was diagnosed with cancer, leaving her holding the bag to take care of her. Georgia Lemmon was tough, though. She survived *that* time."

"But it came back," Forrest guessed.

She nodded.

"What about her deadbeat dad?"

She shook her head.

No wonder Rae had decided that she didn't need a husband to have a family. Not after the example her father had given her.

But that propensity to take off on a sick mate wasn't exclusive to male partners. While Forrest had been working with physical therapists so that he would be able to walk again, his fiancée had taken off. He'd gotten a text.

Sorry, I didn't sign up for this.

Newly engaged, they hadn't worked on their vows yet, but it was clear that she wouldn't have included "in sickness and in health" in hers. And apparently Rae's dad hadn't in his either.

"Could it be her father?" Bellamy asked. "Could his be the body you found in the backyard? Maybe he didn't take off after all."

Forrest shook his head. "This body was like the chief's sister—female and looks as though someone tried to preserve her, too."

Bellamy shuddered again.

Donovan tightened his arm around his wife and assured her, "Forrest will find the sick bastard who did it."

His brother had more faith in him than Forrest probably deserved. He didn't even have a clue right now—

just those weird metallic things he'd found and had sent off to the lab.

"I'm worried about Rae," Bellamy said with concern darkening her dark eyes even more. "How is she?"

"Stubborn," Forrest automatically replied.

Bellamy's lips curved into a slight smile. "You're getting to know my best friend well."

Not well enough.

Not as well as he would have liked. He wished again that he'd kissed her. But that was a line he could not cross—for both their sakes.

He could not be distracted right now, not when he had a case—or cases—to solve.

"I don't know her at all," Forrest said. "And she won't talk to me. She won't answer my questions." Like what was going on with her, and why she was scared.

She had seemed afraid of him, but she had no reason to fear him…unless she was hiding something from him. Like the killer.

Bellamy tensed and pulled away from Donovan. "What questions could you have for Rae? You can't suspect her. You can't think that she has anything to do with the murders."

"Of course he doesn't think that," Donovan answered for him.

Forrest frowned at his brother. "I don't want to think that, but I can tell she's holding something back." Or at least that was the way he'd felt that morning when she'd been so anxious to get rid of him.

Maybe she'd just been busy getting ready for work and all. But Forrest had sensed something else—

something that had to do with him or at least with the investigation.

"It's hard for Rae to trust people," Bellamy said. "It's hard for her to let anyone in."

"Sounds like someone else I know," Donovan said with a grin at his brother. "This guy has a problem trusting people, too."

"I guess that would come with the territory of being a detective," Bellamy mused.

Donovan shook his head. "That's not the only reason."

Shannon was one of the reasons. Donovan knew that Forrest had lost more than his job when he'd been shot. He must have shared *that* with his bride, because she sighed and murmured, "Of course." Then she reached out and grabbed Forrest's hand. "I'm sorry."

"I'm not," he said, and for maybe the first time since he'd received that text, he meant it. "Better I find out before we were married." And losing her hadn't upset him nearly as much as it should have, if he'd truly loved her like their brother Dallas had loved his late wife. His loss was really a loss. Ivy had been awesome. Shannon, on the other hand, hadn't been whom he'd thought she was.

Bellamy sighed again but nodded in agreement.

"You're better off without her," Donovan heartily agreed. "She was selfish. You deserve someone better, someone like Bellamy."

She smiled and leaned back against her husband. "Or like Rae," she added as she arched her dark brows.

Forrest snorted. "She's made it clear she has no interest in me."

But for a second there this morning he'd thought she'd been staring at his mouth as intently as he'd been staring at hers. That she'd leaned forward as he'd leaned down.

That she'd been as attracted to him as he was to her. But then she'd jerked back. And that look on her beautiful face had been so fearful.

Of what?

Him?

Donovan's heart rate quickened as the door closed behind his brother. "Are you mad at me?" he anxiously asked his bride.

"You shouldn't have kept that news from me," Bellamy said. "You should have told me about Forrest finding the body in Rae's backyard."

"Yes," he agreed. Yet the pang that struck his heart wasn't of regret but of concern when he remembered how tired she'd been the past couple of days. He'd been so damn worried about her and the baby.

And that sense of helplessness that had gripped him then gripped him again. He wanted to be able to help her through this pregnancy, but the only thing he could do was try to protect her, to protect *them.* He closed his arms around her—around them both—and held her tightly.

She sighed and leaned against his chest. They were so close that she must have sensed his protectiveness. "You don't have to worry about me. I'm tough. You know that."

"Yes, I do," he agreed with a ragged sigh. "I just didn't want you worrying about Rae."

"I always worry about Rae," Bellamy said with a ragged sigh of her own.

"She's tough, too," Donovan reminded her.

"I know. She's been through so much already, though, and that body turning up in her backyard…" She tensed in his arms. "What if it had been out there as long as the chief's sister was missing? Rae and I used to play in that yard…" She shivered despite the warmth of the day.

Donovan rubbed his hands down her back, trying to warm away her chill. But he suspected the only thing that would put them all at ease would be catching this killer. It was a damn good thing he'd come back.

"Do you think Forrest could be right?" he asked her. "Do you think Rae could know more than she's admitting?"

Bellamy pushed her palms against his chest and pulled away from his embrace. "Absolutely not. Rae can't have anything to do with those murders."

"But could she have some idea who might have committed them?"

"If she did, she would tell Forrest or the chief," Bellamy insisted. "She's going to law school because she wants to help stop some of the crime going on in Whisperwood. She would never protect a killer."

"Not even if that person was a friend?" he asked. "Or a relative?"

"The only person Rae would break the law to protect would be Connor," Bellamy said, "and that sweet baby has nothing to do with any of this."

Donovan smiled. "Of course not."

"And neither does Rae."

Bellamy had known the other woman since kindergarten, so she knew her well. But Donovan knew his brother very well. Usually Forrest's instincts about a case were right—not so much when it came to women, though.

So which was it? Was he seeing Rae Lemmon as a suspect or as a romantic interest?

No matter which, after what Forrest had been through with that flaky fiancée of his, he was unlikely ever to trust her. And Rae didn't trust any man.

Yeah, it was good that he and Bellamy had come home—if only to keep the peace between Bellamy's best friend and his brother.

Dropping Connor at day care that morning had been harder for Rae than it usually was. And it was usually very hard. But letting him out of her sight after what had happened last night had been especially difficult.

And spending all of these hours away from him, stuck at her desk in a windowless room at the law firm, had made her physically ill. Her stomach churned with anxiety and fear. She just wanted to be with her son, to make sure that he was safe. She knew that she didn't need to worry, though.

The day care was very well staffed with maternal types who were even more overprotective than she was, including the male owner, Bob McCauley, who was a former football player. Nobody would be able to get one of the babies past him without one hell of a fight. But even knowing that…

She couldn't shake her fear for her son. Had she put him in danger that morning, talking to Forrest Colton? She never should have opened the door to him.

Would her note writer punish her for disregarding his warning?

She wanted to be with Connor, but maybe he was safer at the day care than he would be with her. Bob would protect him more effectively than she could. Maybe that was why she was still at work this late.

Sure, she'd had piles of research for a pending case for one of the partners. She could have gotten through it faster, though, if she hadn't been so distracted.

She had been so distracted that she hadn't even realized what time it was…until she noticed the digital numbers on the corner of her computer monitor. She gasped and then sucked in a breath as the sound echoed eerily in her small office. No other noise drifted beneath the door like it usually did.

Everybody else must have already left for the day. And she should have, too. Bob wouldn't be worried; the day care center had a second shift for parents who worked later or had classes after work, like she did a couple of nights a week. But now that she knew what time it was, she was anxious to leave the office.

Especially since it felt so forebodingly empty.

She shut down her computer and gathered up her stuff, shoving it inside the purse with the note and lock of hair she'd sealed in a plastic bag, like evidence.

Should she have given it to Forrest?

The thought lifted goose bumps on her skin, though, as a chill rushed through her blood. She couldn't risk it—no matter how much she wanted the person who'd threatened her son to be caught.

And the killer.

Were they the same?

They must have been or why the threat? Only the killer would want Forrest out of the way. Well, she and the killer. Even if she hadn't received the threat, she wouldn't want Forrest Colton around her. She had too much going on—she was way too busy to deal with him and that annoying attraction she felt for him. And that was all it was: an annoyance.

That annoyance surged through her now as she threw her purse over her shoulder and stepped out of her office into the dark hallway. Like her office, it had no windows, and someone had shut off the lights already.

Hadn't they noticed the light under her door? Hadn't they realized that she was still at work? Or had that been the reason for shutting off the lights? To spook her even more?

Goose bumps rose on her skin as that chill chased through her again. But would the person who'd broken into her house know where she worked, as well?

Whisperwood was a small enough town and so gossipy that everybody knew everybody else's business. It would be easy enough for anyone to track her down at home and at work.

She hurried down the hall toward the elevators,

rushing past the closed doors of other offices along the way. A loud *thump* emanated from beneath one of those closed doors, and she gasped in shock at hearing the sound. Then a giggle followed her gasp, and her fear eased.

Apparently she wasn't the only one working late… although the *thump* and the giggling didn't sound much like work.

The doorknob to the closest office rattled as the door opened slightly. Kenneth Dawson peered out through the crack, his thin blond hair slightly mussed. "Oh, Rae, I didn't realize you were still here."

Which explained why the lights had been shut off. With her office farther down the hall than his, he wouldn't have noticed the light under her door.

"I'm leaving now," she assured him.

"Worked late like I am," he said.

His flushed face made it look like he had been working out—physically and not mentally.

"My wife brought me dinner," he added with a smile.

Rae smiled and nodded. "Oh, that was very sweet of her."

"Yes," he agreed, but he didn't open his door any farther and offer to introduce his wife to Rae, which was odd since he'd once invited her to join them for dinner at his house.

Of course Rae was always in a hurry to leave and get Connor from day care, so he probably didn't expect her to want to linger. And she didn't.

"Enjoy your dinner," she said. "Good night." And

she rushed off toward the elevators again. An elevator car came quickly—since everybody else had probably already left the building for the night. She stepped inside and as the doors began to close, that giggle rang out again.

Mrs. Dawson sounded so happy and youthful. Rae wished she would have taken the time to meet her. But she needed to get to Connor. So she rushed from the building, to her SUV and then to the day care center, and as she did, she kept glancing around her, checking for anyone looking at her, watching her.

But nobody and nothing stuck out to her. Of course she was learning to be a lawyer, not a cop—just as Forrest Colton had pointed out to her. She didn't know how to accurately assess who might pose a threat to her or to Connor.

"Everything okay?" Bob asked as the burly middle-aged man carried the baby carrier to the car for her.

She nodded.

"I heard about another body turning up out at your place," he said.

She shuddered.

"If you need anything…"

She thought about telling him about the threat, but like her friends, he would probably also want her to call the police. And the last thing she needed was the police—particularly Detective Forrest Colton—coming around her place again.

Hopefully he had concluded his search quickly that morning and was long gone. When she pulled into her driveway a short while later, she didn't notice any vehicles. But a light did glow inside the house.

Had one just been left on? Or was someone inside?

Leaving Connor in the back seat in his carrier, she headed cautiously toward the house. The door was shut, but behind the curtains pulled across the windows, a shadow moved. Someone was inside her house.

Forrest?

Or the person who'd snuck in last night to threaten her son?

Chapter 7

Forrest hadn't expected a warm welcome. Hell, he hadn't expected a welcome at all—just questions and confusion and pain.

So much pain.

But neither man cried. They hadn't when he'd notified them of Patrice's death either. Her brother and her widowed father had been in shock then, so he hadn't asked them many questions. That was why he'd returned tonight, to talk to them after they'd had some time to process the news of their loss. But they were more inclined to ask their own questions than they were to answer his.

"What are you doing to find her killer?" her father, Atticus Eccleston, asked.

"Is her murder your primary focus?" her brother asked. "Or do you only care about the old bodies?"

Forrest furrowed his brow in confusion. "What?"

"We heard all the news reports about you," the father explained. "That you're a cold-case detective."

"My last assignment with the Austin Police Department was in the cold-case unit," Forrest admitted. That was his position when he'd been shot. "But I worked in the homicide unit for a long time before that."

And he'd been so damn good at solving murders that they'd moved him to the cold-case unit. Bragging about his past wouldn't give these guys what they needed. Only finding Patrice's killer would give them the justice and closure they wanted.

"Stopping this killer is my top priority," he assured them. Before he killed again.

An image of Rae's face, pale with fear, flashed through his mind. With a killer on the loose, she had every reason to be afraid, but a feeling nagged at him, making him wonder if she had another reason. But what?

"It's too late for my sister," Ian Eccleston said. "Too late to do anything to save her or bring her back." But still he didn't cry; his face just flushed with rage. And his fists were clenched, as if he was tempted to take a swing at Forrest.

He'd been attacked during plenty of other investigations, but usually the suspect tried to fight him, not the family member of a victim.

"I am very sorry for your loss," he told them both—as he had the other night. They hadn't acknowledged his comment that night. They'd been too shocked. Too numb.

Unfortunately that numbness had worn off to leave anger and pain.

"We don't want your sympathy," Ian scoffed, and he walked over to open the front door of the house he shared with his father. "We want results. If you can't get them, we'll find the bastard ourselves."

"Give the lab time to process all the evidence from the scene," Forrest said as he stepped out that open door. "And if you remember anything that might help our investigation—"

"We would have already told you," Ian said, and he slammed the door in Forrest's face—just like Rae had that morning.

And both instances had Forrest feeling again like he wasn't being told everything—like these people knew more than they were sharing with him.

He wasn't going to get anything else out of Ian Eccleston. But he might be able to get Rae to tell him more, if her friends were right that she could be trusted.

But then, his experience with Shannon had taught him that it was better to trust no one, at least not with his heart. He was damn sure Rae Lemmon didn't want that anyway, though, or she wouldn't have jerked back before he'd been able to kiss her. Not that he'd any business kissing her.

But her backyard was a murder scene, so he definitely had business with her.

And right now that business was unfinished.

She hadn't known what to do when she'd seen that shadow pass behind her living room curtains. Rae hadn't known if she should call the police.

But before they arrived, the intruder could have

made good on their threat to hurt Connor. Or her. So to protect her son, she'd turned and run back to her vehicle. But when she'd opened the door, someone had stopped her—with a hand on her arm. And she'd screamed in terror...until Bellamy had spoken.

"I'm sorry I scared you," she said again—as she had when she'd first approached Rae on the driveway.

Rae forced a smile. "It's fine. I'm just so tired that I'm jumpy."

"Are you sure you're just tired?" Maggie asked. She'd showed up moments after Rae had with the pizza her sister had been craving. It sat mostly untouched in the middle of the kitchen table.

They had probably already eaten with their significant others and had really bought the pizza for her. But Rae wasn't hungry, not with all of the knots of dread and fear filling her stomach.

"Or is Forrest right and you're scared of something?" Bellamy asked.

She tensed. "Forrest? He talked to you?" she asked. "About me?"

Bellamy nodded.

"He had no right to interrogate you," Rae said. "You're not a suspect and neither am I."

Bellamy glanced down at the table, as if she couldn't meet Rae's eyes.

Horrified, Rae asked, "Am I a suspect?"

Bellamy looked back up now, her gaze intent on Rae's face. "He doesn't think you're a killer, but he thinks you know something you're not telling him."

"Are you interrogating me now?" Rae asked defen-

sively. But now she couldn't meet her friend's eyes.
She jumped up from the table and began to collect
the plates.

Maggie said, "I can get those." But she was holding Connor on her lap, and the both of them looked
so content.

Connor hadn't looked like that last night. He'd looked
terrified. And that terror passed through Rae as she remembered the intruder's threat.

Tears stung her eyes, blurring her vision. She blinked
furiously as she turned away to carry the dishes to
the sink. But someone grabbed her arm, holding her
in place.

"You are scared," Bellamy said.

"A body was found in my backyard," Rae reminded
her. "Of course I would be scared."

"Anybody would be," Maggie agreed with her with
a shudder of revulsion.

But Bellamy shook her head. She'd known Rae too
long and too well. "Not you," she said. "Forrest is right.
There's something else that has rattled you." She narrowed her eyes and tilted her head. "Is it him?"

"H-h-him?" Rae sputtered. "Does he think that?"
Had he guessed that she was attracted to him? Since
she'd just about risen up on tiptoe and pressed her lips
to his, he'd probably guessed—not to mention that she'd
asked him to dance at the wedding a few weeks ago.

Bellamy smiled. "No. Not Forrest. Not after what
his fiancée did to him."

Rae gasped. She hadn't known he was engaged. If

she had, she never would have asked him to dance or nearly kissed him. "What did his fiancée do?"

"Ex-fiancée," Maggie chimed in.

So she'd known about his engagement, too.

"When he got shot, while he was still recovering, she took off with his ring," Bellamy said.

Rae sucked in a breath. "She left him?"

Bellamy nodded. "He had to endure months of physical therapy before he could even walk again, and instead of helping him through that, she took off."

Just like Rae's dad had taken off when her mother had been diagnosed with cancer. She flinched. So it wasn't just men who couldn't be counted on to stick around.

"She hurt him badly when she abandoned him," Bellamy continued. "Not just his heart but his self-esteem. He doesn't think you're into him. He thinks you're lying to him."

"About what?" Rae asked.

"About the killer," Bellamy continued. "He thinks you know something about him, that you're protecting him."

Could it really be the killer who had left that note for her? She'd pretty much already concluded that it had to be, though. Who else would want the detective out of the way, besides her?

"Is that why you're here?" Rae asked. "Do you think that, too?"

"Of course not," Bellamy assured her as she jumped up from the table to put an arm around her. "I told him that the only person you would lie to protect would be Connor."

Rae sucked in a breath and tensed. And Bellamy must have felt that tension. She turned Rae toward her. "That's it, isn't it? Someone has threatened Connor."

Maggie jumped up from the table, too, with the baby cradled protectively in her arms. Both of these women would protect her child as fiercely as she would.

Rae trusted them. Tears rushed to her eyes as she nodded. "Yes." Her voice cracked with the fear that bubbled up inside her. She shouldn't have come back here. But she was glad that she had, glad that Bellamy had been waiting for her.

"Who?" Maggie asked. "Who's threatening you?"

"I don't know," Rae admitted. She grabbed her purse from the counter, where she'd dropped it, and she pulled out the plastic bag containing the note and Connor's hair. "Someone was in the house last night— in Connor's room."

"Why didn't you call the police?" Bellamy asked.

"Because the note told her not to," Maggie pointed out.

"But I should have," Rae admitted. By not calling the police, Rae had let the person get away with what he'd done—breaking in and threatening her son.

"You should have left the minute it happened," Maggie said, and she tightened her arms around the baby as she looked fearfully out the kitchen windows.

She'd been glad her friends had been here, but now she realized that their being here put them in danger, too. A danger that they hadn't even known about, because she hadn't been open and honest with them about what was going on with her.

"You should have come to one of us," Bellamy said.

Rae nodded. "I know but I knew you guys would want me to call the police, that you'd want me to report it. And I was worried that the note writer would come back, that he'd make good on his threat." The tears spilled over, running down her face as sobs bubbled up from her throat.

Bellamy held her tightly. "You and Connor are not going to be alone from now on. We'll protect you. We'll all protect you."

Rae loved her friends too much to put them in danger, especially now with Bellamy pregnant and Maggie so happy. She pulled back from Bellamy's embrace. "No, you won't. I'll call the police."

It was their job to protect people. Of course their presence would also put her and her son in danger.

More danger.

They were already in danger.

"Call Forrest," Bellamy told her as she drew her cell from her pocket…as if she intended to call if Rae refused.

She knew what she had to do, what she should have done right after she'd found the note. But she'd been so scared then, so terrified that someone had so easily gotten to her son. Without protection, that was bound to happen again.

Yet she couldn't help but worry that Forrest's involvement would put them in more danger, not just from the killer but from that attraction she felt for him.

She couldn't fall for another man who wasn't going to stick around when she needed him.

And once Forrest solved these murder cases, he would leave Whisperwood. The hurricane was the only reason he'd been here in the first place.

"Chief, Chief," reporters called out from the television screen that sat on the bureau at the foot of his bed.

He—along with all of the other viewers—watched Archer Thompson turn toward the reporters gathered outside the Whisperwood Police Department.

"Was Elliot Corgan an innocent man? Or is there another serial killer on the loose?"

As part of his plea deal, Elliot Corgan's name had not been released as the Whisperwood killer. That had probably been more his family's doing than his, though. They hadn't wanted anyone to know the biggest landowners in Whisperwood had a killer among them.

He snorted. Elliot hadn't been their only disgrace, though. Even the younger generation had proved to be a disappointment. But Elliot had definitely been their biggest.

Why hadn't he just claimed the sheriff's sister as one of his victims? Then all of this would have been done. But hers wasn't the only body that had turned up. Why the hell couldn't the dead stay buried?

He focused on the chief again, who declined to answer any questions. "This is an ongoing investigation," he said, "so I'm not at liberty to comment on it."

"Is that because you've turned over the investigation to Forrest Colton?" another reporter asked. "Why did you do that, Chief? Because it was too close to home for you?"

Archer turned fully toward the cameras and the television viewers now. The man was older, but age didn't affect his tall body. He stood straight and strong. "I did that because Forrest Colton gets results. He closes cases. He finds killers. And he will find this one."

Not if the killer found him first and got rid of him.

Chapter 8

Forrest was in the morgue. Again.

Over the course of his law-enforcement career, he'd spent entirely too much time in the morgue. Other detectives accepted the coroner's report without question. Forrest wanted to see the wounds himself; it helped him connect to the victim and to the killer.

What kind of killer preserved his victims as the chief's sister and the body of the woman in Rae's backyard had been preserved?

And why not Patrice?

Had there just not been enough time for him to process her body as he had the others?

Or didn't he have the energy anymore?

No. The bruises around her neck certainly showed

the strength of her killer. He didn't lack energy. So it must have been time he'd lacked.

Poor Patrice.

She had been so young, so vital. The sheriff's sister and the other victim had once been young, too. The killer had tried to keep them young with the way he'd preserved them. But they had died long ago.

Unlike Patrice.

Since she was the most recent victim, her murder should be the easiest to solve. But Forrest was drawn to the other body, to the one he'd found in Rae's backyard.

Hell, he was just drawn to Rae and to her son. And he had no damn idea why. He had a case to work, which was something that, after the shooting, he'd thought he would never have the opportunity to do again. This was his chance to prove himself, to prove that he was still capable of performing the job he loved.

So he couldn't afford any distractions like Rae and her beautiful brown eyes and her curvy figure and her soft skin and her full lips.

Lips he wished he'd kissed.

"See anything I missed?" the coroner asked, her voice sharp with sarcasm.

Forrest sighed. "That's not what I'm looking for," he assured her. "And as I told you, you didn't need to be here." In fact he would have preferred to be alone, so he could think. But even with her present, he'd been able to think only of Rae Lemmon, of how she'd looked that morning.

Scared.

Was that because she'd guessed he was about to kiss her? Was that what had scared her?

He was a little scared of how badly he'd wanted to kiss her, of how much of an attraction he felt for her.

"I want the killer caught, too," the coroner said.

"I know," he said.

"I have daughters this age," she continued with a catch in her voice. "I hate to think of them out there with a killer."

Maybe that was why he kept thinking of Rae—because she was so alone out there, where he'd already found one body. Well, she had Connor. But he was no protection. He needed her; he was totally dependent on her.

She had to stay safe. Didn't she realize that?

"Tell them to be careful," he advised.

She snorted. "They will tell you that I already nag them quite enough. They are careful. But these women probably thought they were being careful, too."

He nodded. They probably had.

Just like Rae Lemmon thought she was being careful, that she could take care of herself and her son without any help. Hopefully she had at least reached out to her friends, since she clearly had no intention of reaching out to him.

And his reaching out, albeit theoretically, to these victims hadn't given him any new clues to the killer's identity. "You be careful, too," Forrest advised the medical examiner. "I'm sorry you came down here for nothing."

She sighed. "I wish you had found something I missed," she said. "Something that would lead us to this monster."

He nodded. But he had nothing else to say, so he turned to leave. He'd just stepped into the hall and closed the door when the cell in his pocket began to vibrate.

If it was the coroner, she would have just opened the door and called him back. It had to be someone else, so he drew out the cell. But he didn't recognize the number on the screen. It could have been a reporter; several of them had been calling him to comment on the investigation, especially since they weren't getting much out of the chief.

He stared down at the screen, though, hesitating before pressing that decline button. Something compelled him to press the accept button instead.

"Colton here," he said.

"Uhh…" a soft voice stammered in his ear. "This—this is Rae Lemmon."

He hadn't imagined that fear this morning. He heard it now in her voice. "What's wrong?" he asked.

"I—I need to talk to you," she said.

"Are you home?" he asked.

"Yes," she said. "And my friends refuse to leave until you get here."

She was definitely in danger.

"Should I send out a police car?"

"No!" she quickly rejected the offer. "Just you. Please come alone."

Come alone?

He had agreed to that stipulation before—when a potential witness had set up a meeting with him. That *witness* had started shooting the minute he'd turned up to the warehouse where they'd agreed to meet. The "come alone" stipulation had been the trap that had nearly taken his life, as well as his livelihood and so much else.

But this was Rae, so once again he found himself agreeing. "I'm on my way." He clicked off the cell but the sound of her voice, with the fear cracking it, still rang in his ears. He tried rushing up the stairs, from the basement to the lobby, but his leg had stiffened up and refused to bend, forcing him to hobble. Maybe it was because it had been a long day of being on his feet, or maybe it was because he needed the reminder—the warning—to be careful.

Once she was alone, Rae wished her friends would come back. But she was the one who'd convinced them to leave, who'd assured them that Forrest was on his way and she would not be alone for long. But every second that they were gone felt like an hour, an hour of her tensing with fear over every creak of the house and every whisper of the wind outside the windows.

Even Connor had left her alone with her thoughts, since he'd fallen asleep in his crib. He must have forgotten all about the night before. She wished she could forget, too, but that note and that lock of hair would haunt her for a long time.

She held them in her hand now, still sealed in that plastic bag. She couldn't wait to hand them over to Forrest Colton. Maybe that was why she was so on edge waiting for him to arrive. She was scared to be alone, but her senses hummed with excitement at the thought of seeing him again.

Lights flashed in her windows as a vehicle turned

into her driveway. Her pulse leaped. But she wasn't afraid that her intruder had returned. She doubted he would have just driven up to her house, since he hadn't done that the night before. She knew who had arrived, and it was why her pulse leaped, why her skin heated, why her heart pounded.

Forrest was here.

She met him at the door. He must have jumped out of his SUV before he'd even shut it off, because he'd taken no time to get from it to her porch despite his limp.

"I thought your friends were going to stay until I got here," he said. "I would have driven faster if I knew they were gone."

"They just left," she assured him as he stepped inside the house. He couldn't have arrived any faster than he had—even if he'd been at his parents' ranch where he'd been staying since his volunteering with the Cowboy Heroes had brought him home to Whisperwood. But she suspected he hadn't been there, since he was still wearing the dress pants, with his boots, that he'd had on that morning. If he'd been home to the ranch, he probably would have changed into jeans.

She closed the door behind him and, with her hands trembling, turned the lock. Locking the door had done no good the night before, though.

"They should have waited for me to get here," he said. "Are you okay? What's going on?"

His concern touched her—so much that tears overwhelmed her, filling her eyes and her throat. In reply to his questions, she handed him the plastic bag.

"What the hell…?" he murmured as he stared down at the handwritten note.

"I found this lying on my pillow last night," she managed to say around the emotion choking her.

"And the hair?" He stared at her now, as if trying to see where it had been cut.

"Connor's," she said. "I woke up because he started screaming. When I was in the nursery with him, I heard someone walking out of the house and closing the door. I ran back into my bedroom for my cell phone, and I found this." She shuddered at the memory.

"And then you didn't call the police to report the break-in," he said. "And that's why you also tried to get rid of me in the morning."

"I want to protect my son," she said.

"That's why you should have called right away," Forrest admonished her. "Or told me when I arrived this morning. We could have checked for fingerprints and for signs of a break-in."

"I couldn't find any," she admitted.

"Hadn't you locked the door?"

She bristled with defensiveness. "Of course I did." She hadn't always, but after he'd found that body in her backyard, she'd checked the lock twice before she'd gone to bed that night.

He was looking at the lock now, inspecting it from the inside and then from the outside, after he unlocked and opened the door. "Nobody forced it. Do you have a spare key hidden outside?"

She nodded and gestured at the gardenia plant. "Under the flowerpot."

He studied the pot now, where dirt had spilled over the rim of it onto the porch. Before he touched it, he pulled the sleeves of his suit coat over his hands. Then he tipped it and peered beneath it. "There's no key."

"There was," she insisted. But her head began to pound as she tried to remember the last time she'd seen it. "Bellamy might have left it out when she'd used it earlier." That was how she had probably let herself in, unless Forrest's team had left her doors unlocked. "She has her own, though, so she might not have used it. She's the only one who knows it's there besides me. And I always use the one on my key chain." When she remembered to lock the door at all.

Forrest snorted. "A flowerpot next to the door? It's the first place I'd look if I was trying to get inside."

Heat rushed to her face as she realized it hadn't been the best hiding spot. But until recently crime hadn't been much of a concern in Whisperwood—at least not that she could remember. She wouldn't have been much older than Connor was when Elliot Corgan had been killing women.

He was dead now, though. He couldn't be responsible for these murders.

It had been there a long time, and her property was close to Corgan ranch land. He could have buried one of his victims in her backyard.

Forrest touched his hand to the small of her back and guided her back into the house. The heat of his touch warmed her again. He closed the door behind them.

"You need to get your locks changed," he said. Then

a curse slipped out of his lips. "Hell, you need to leave this place. It's a crime scene."

She glanced around the place, but like when she'd returned home earlier, she saw no signs of his search—no evidence of his finding any evidence inside her house. "Did you find something?" she asked. She then shuddered before asking, "Blood? DNA?"

He shook his head. "Nothing to indicate that a person was murdered inside the house."

She uttered a ragged sigh of relief. "Then it's not a crime scene."

He held up the plastic bag. "It is. Do you have any idea who left you the note?"

She shook her head now. "No, no idea."

He stared at her, his hazel eyes narrowed as if he considered her a suspect. She hadn't left herself the damn note, though now, like the note's writer, she was wishing the detective was gone.

"What about you?" she asked. "You're the one he wants out of the way, so you must have some idea who it is."

He grimaced. "I wish I had an idea, a suspect, something." A curse slipped out between his lips. "I'm sorry."

She wished she could blame the note on him. But he wasn't the one who'd threatened her. None of this was his fault—except for how he made her feel.

She had been so focused lately on just being a mother and a student and a worker that she'd nearly forgotten she was a woman, too. He'd reminded her, which was probably why he irritated her so much. Or maybe he wouldn't irritate her so much if he actually returned the attraction. For a moment that morning she'd thought he'd been about to kiss her, but she must have imagined that, because he was all business now.

"You were smart to seal this in a bag," he said. "I'll have it dusted for prints."

"Maybe you'll find some on Connor's crib, too," she suggested. "He must have leaned over it to snip that piece of hair from his head." Tears rushed to her eyes again as she relived the horror of how close somebody had been to her son, how easily he could have been hurt or worse.

"Is he okay?" Forrest asked, and his free hand moved to her shoulder.

The weight of it felt good, felt comforting somehow, while also unsettling her. She nodded. "Yes, he's fine. He's sleeping soundly, while I don't think I'll ever be able to sleep again."

"Not here," Forrest agreed. "You need to get out of here. Go stay with Bellamy and Donovan or Maggie and Jonah."

She shook her head. "That's not an option."

"They're your friends. They would let you stay with them if you asked."

"I don't have to ask," she said. "They already offered."

"Then—" he glanced around the floor "—where are your bags?"

"I'm not going to impose on my friends," she said. "Not with a baby who still doesn't sleep through the night."

"I don't think they would mind," he assured her.

"They wouldn't," she agreed. "But I would. I don't want anyone else losing sleep because of me or my son."

"Then you need to book a room at a hotel—preferably one with good security."

Heat rushed to her face. With the costs of day care and law school, she didn't have an extra dime to spare. She couldn't afford to stay in a hotel with bad security, let alone one with good. But she was too proud to admit that to him, so she just murmured, "I can't."

"Then I'll stay here," he offered.

A twinge of panic gripped her heart. "No. You can't. The note writer wants you out of the way."

"Yeah," Forrest agreed. "So he can terrorize you. That's why I should be here."

Scared, she shook her head as tears rushed to her eyes again. "No. You can't. It's too dangerous."

"It's too dangerous for you and Connor to be here alone," he said. His hand on her shoulder turned her toward him and then pulled her closer. "I will protect you."

But she had a feeling that he might be the one from whom she needed the most protection—because she wanted him so badly.

His hand moved from her shoulder to her face. His fingers brushed across her cheek and along her jaw before he tipped up her face. "I will keep you safe."

Staring at his handsome features, at the intensity in his hazel eyes, Rae felt anything but safe. She felt everything…a desire she hadn't felt in so long, if ever.

His eyes darkened, and he suddenly lowered his head to hers. But he paused—with just a breath between their lips—and she was the one who rose up on tiptoe, who pressed her mouth to his.

A jolt shot from her lips straight to her heart, making it pound madly against her breast. His lips were still—for a moment—before they moved hungrily over hers. He kissed her with a passion she hadn't suspected him to be capable of, that she hadn't expected that she was capable of feeling until it coursed through her. She raised her arms and threw them around his neck, holding his head down to hers—holding his long, tense body against hers.

A kiss had never affected her as much, had never made her want as much, as she wanted Forrest Colton—and not just for protection.

What the hell is she doing?

Hadn't she heeded the warning at all? The note had specifically said to get rid of the detective. Maybe she hadn't called Detective Colton out to the house, but she hadn't thrown him out like she had the last time he'd showed up, that morning.

And with the way their shadows moved behind the curtains, she had no intention of getting rid of him. She held him as if she never intended to let him go.

And that wasn't good. It might wind up costing her so much.

So damn much.

Chapter 9

Who was in the most danger? The baby? Rae? Or Forrest? He wasn't sure. While the threat had been made against little Connor, Forrest wasn't as worried about the baby as he was about himself.

But he had a job to do—at least that was his excuse for staying at Rae's house. It had also been his excuse for pulling away from her earlier that evening, when everything inside him had been urging him to lift her up in his arms and carry her off to her bed. Then he'd remembered that if he'd tried, his leg would have probably folded beneath their combined weights and sent them both crashing to the floor.

Embarrassed and angry at the thought, he'd pulled away from her then.

Her face flushed with embarrassment, she'd stumbled back and murmured, "I'm sorry."

"*I'm* sorry," he'd said, correcting her. He'd started to kiss her first—before he'd stopped and waited to make sure she'd wanted this, too. But even though she'd closed the distance between them and pressed her lips to his first, he had been taking advantage of her—of her fear and vulnerability.

"I'm sorry," he'd repeated. "I know the only reason I'm staying here is to protect you and Connor."

And he couldn't do that if he was distracted with his desire for her. He'd gone into the nursery then to stand guard over her son, and she'd gone to bed.

Alone.

His body tightened at the thought of Rae, tangled in her sheets, wearing only the old T-shirt that molded to her curves. She'd looked so sexy in it, so sexy that he couldn't help but imagine how she would look out of it, with nothing but the flush of desire on her skin. She had seemed to want him as much as he'd wanted her.

So maybe he hadn't been taking advantage of her vulnerability. But he had been neglecting his job, which was to protect her and her son.

From the killer?

That had to be who had left the threat. Who else would want him out of the way? Besides Rae? She hadn't been happy to see him the past couple of days— until earlier tonight. Tonight she had been relieved when he'd showed up, but only because she was afraid.

That was why she'd kissed him. Out of fear and maybe gratitude. She couldn't actually be interested in him; that would mean that she was willing to take on another responsibility for her already overburdened shoulders. Shannon hadn't wanted the responsibility of caring for someone with an injury, and she'd once loved him. Why would Rae want to deal with his disability?

Not that he saw a future with her—with them. He wasn't sure he was even going to stay in Whisperwood after he solved his case or cases. He wasn't sure yet if the murders were connected or not.

Hell, he wasn't sure of anything anymore.

What the hell was he even thinking by staying here, trying to protect them? He should have called in a uniformed officer for that duty.

But Rae had been so frightened…

That he hadn't been able to leave. And so he stood watch in the nursery now.

Connor had been sleeping peacefully, just a whisper of breath escaping his little nose and rosebud lips. But a soft cry slipped through them now, and the baby tensed in his crib.

Forrest glanced toward the doorway. He didn't want to wake up Rae, didn't really want to see her wearing only that T-shirt, or he was going to wind up in more trouble than if the intruder attempted to get inside again. So he reached inside the crib, slid his hands beneath the little body and lifted Connor from his bed.

The baby blinked open bleary eyes and stared up at Forrest. His mouth opened, but instead of letting out a louder scream, a little burp slipped between his lips. And a little bubble floated out.

Forrest chuckled. "A little gassy, huh?"

Those little rosebud lips curved into what looked like a smile, but that was probably just gas, too. Forrest found himself smiling back anyway. Then his palm grew damp where he cupped the little guy's pajama bottom, and he swallowed a groan. The baby was wet.

He needed a diaper change, or he was probably going to start crying for real.

Forrest glanced toward the doorway again. Maybe it would be better for Rae to handle this. Forrest wasn't squeamish—not after all of the crime scenes he'd investigated—but he had never changed a diaper before.

How hard could it be, though?

And with Bellamy expecting his niece or nephew, he was going to need to learn—if he ever intended to help out with babysitting.

Connor's face twisted into a little grimace, as if he'd just noticed the wetness, too, and another cry slipped out of his lips.

"I've got this," Forrest assured him. "I'll change you." At least he would give it a try.

He carried the little guy over to the piece of furniture that looked like a low dresser that had been painted blue and decorated with sheep. The pad on the top of it also had little sheep on it. A couple of disposable diapers had been left on top of it, as well. Forrest breathed a sigh of relief that he wouldn't have to deal with pins—just tape and the little guy's flailing feet in those damp pajamas.

Forrest unsnapped the onesie thing but getting Connor's feet out with all his kicking was not an easy task.

He didn't want to hurt him. "You gotta help me out here, buddy," he murmured. "We have to get this thing off you."

He was able to tug on the pajamas until Connor's kicking legs slipped out. Then he ripped off the sodden diaper, pulled it from beneath him and wadded it up before opening the blue pail next to the changing table and dropping it inside. "Okay, we got that nasty thing off."

Forrest reached for the wipes and the powder. After cleaning him, he sprinkled some powder, which wafted up like a cloud. He sneezed, and something gurgled out of the baby again, something that sounded like a giggle.

Probably just gas again. But Forrest smiled down at him anyway. "You think this is funny?" he asked.

The little feet kicked again.

Forrest slid a clean diaper beneath him and secured it around him with the tape on each side. Or he hoped he had secured it. When he lifted Connor from the table, the diaper didn't fall off, so he hadn't done too badly.

Except that he didn't know where the clean pajamas were. "Do you need new pj's?" Forrest asked as he cradled the baby against his chest. The little body was warm, and so was the house and the night outside it. He wasn't going to freeze if Forrest couldn't find him dry clothes. But a twinge of guilt struck him that maybe he wasn't doing this right.

Connor gurgled again and now his little fists flailed against Forrest's chest. He wasn't fighting to get away, though; he was just restless and wide-awake.

"How do I get you back to sleep?" Forrest wondered aloud. "Do I sing? I don't know any lullabies."

But to be a good uncle, he should probably learn some. At the moment all that came to his mind were the words to the old Guns N' Roses song "Sweet Child o' Mine."

As he sang, heat rushed to his face—not that singing to Connor should have embarrassed him, but he had a sensation that the baby wasn't the only one listening to him. And this time when he glanced to the doorway, someone stood there in that old, thin T-shirt.

"Don't stop on my account," she said, her voice husky with sleep. "This is the first time I've heard a heavy metal lullaby."

His face grew even hotter. "It was the only song I could think of." But now he could think of nothing but her looking so damn beautiful and sounding so damn sexy with that sleep in her voice.

Sweet child of mine...
The words to the song, sung in his deep voice, resonated throughout her head and her heart.
Sweet child of mine...
Connor wasn't his child. But he was caring for him like he was. She'd watched while he'd changed the baby's diaper and then sung him back to sleep. While she had miraculously managed to fall asleep even after that kiss they'd shared, she'd awakened the minute she'd heard Connor's cry.

And fear had pierced her heart like the blade of a sharp knife. Then she'd heard the deep murmur of a familiar voice, and her fear had subsided. Forrest Colton was here, protecting them.

But he'd done even more than that; he'd taken care of Connor in a way no one had but her since the baby's birth. He'd changed him and cuddled with him and sung to him.

Warmth flooded Rae's heart, which felt as if it had swelled in her chest, as she stared at the two of them: the big man with the tiny baby clasped against his heart. This warmth wasn't just for her son.

Forrest was so much more than he'd seemed when they'd first met. When he'd turned down her invitation to dance, she'd thought he was cold and bitter, but that wasn't who he was at all. There was nothing cold and bitter about him now as he gently cradled the baby.

She'd thought she'd wanted to do this alone, that being a single parent was the best for her and for her son. She didn't want Connor to have a father who would just let him down and leave like hers had. But now she'd gotten a glimpse of what it could be like if Connor had a father—for him and for her.

Now the warmth spread to her face with embarrassment that she was fantasizing about a man she barely knew. She liked his brothers a lot, but just because his last name was Colton, too, didn't mean that he was a good man. There were other branches of the Colton family tree, branches that were as dangerous as the Corgans had proved to be.

But Forrest was a lawman, so she doubted that he was at all like his dangerous relatives. At least he wasn't a physical danger to her. But emotionally…

He was making her long for something she'd already given up on ever finding: love. A man who would stay.

He was only here because it was his job, though.

"I didn't realize diaper duty was part of the service," she said.

"If you'd known, would you have called me last night, when the intruder left the note?" he asked.

She shivered as she remembered how different last night had been from this one. She'd been so terrified—so alone. Maybe it wasn't all that different, though. She was scared tonight, too, but of what she was beginning to feel for Forrest Colton.

Attraction and something deeper, something that would cause her pain if she gave in to it, but she couldn't—she *wouldn't*—give in to her feelings. He wasn't even sticking around Whisperwood. He was only here because of the hurricane, because he was a volunteer for the Cowboy Heroes. He probably would have been gone already if he hadn't been hired to help out the Whisperwood PD with the murder investigation.

Rae had to protect her heart. She couldn't be like her mother, who'd fallen for a man who hadn't stuck around. While Georgia hadn't realized that about Beau Lemmon at the time she'd met him, Rae knew Forrest wasn't staying.

"I'm not sure I should have called you at all," she admitted. She knew she definitely shouldn't have kissed him—because now she wanted to kiss him again, so badly.

"You're worried about the threat," he surmised. "That the intruder will come back and make good on it."

She nodded. But with Connor clasped in Forrest's arm, he was safe. She was the one in danger, because she wanted to be clasped in Forrest's arms, too.

"I'll make sure you and Connor have twenty-four-hour protection," he assured her. "There's no way the person who left that note will hurt either of you."

He sounded so determined that some relief eased the tension that had been gripping her. "Thank you," she said.

His face flushed. "I'm just doing my job."

After she'd kissed him, he probably wanted to make that clear to her, so that she didn't misconstrue his protection as affection for her or for Connor. But the way he'd kissed her...

And the way he held her son, so gently.

She shook off the wistfulness that had suddenly come over her. "I know," she assured him, but her lips curved into a teasing smile. "Although, I'm not sure diaper duty is part of being a detective."

He smiled back at her. "I didn't want him to wake you up."

She couldn't help but wonder why. Out of consideration? Or because he hadn't wanted to see her again?

"I—I should call in a replacement for me for the morning," he said. Clearly he didn't intend to be her twenty-four-hour protector. He had a job to do, and babysitting her and Connor was not part of that job.

He carefully placed the sleeping baby back in his crib before pulling his cell phone from his pocket. "I'll make my call outside," he said. "So I don't wake him again."

But he hesitated over leaving the room, as if reluctant to pass her in the doorway. When he neared her, his body tensed, and he sucked in a breath and held it.

She stared up at him as he passed her, and his hazel eyes darkened with desire. Or maybe that was just wishful thinking on her part, because he continued past her as if she hadn't tempted him at all.

But she was tempted to follow him out, to kiss him again. The crib sheets rustled as Connor moved in his bed and a little cry slipped through his lips. His cry brought Rae to her senses. She couldn't throw herself at Forrest again; he obviously didn't want her.

"I want her," Forrest Colton said.

The chief blinked away the bleariness of sleep, jerked fully awake and focused on the cell in his hand. "What?" he asked.

"I want Rae Lemmon to have around-the-clock protection," Forrest said.

Maybe that was what he'd said the first time, but Archer had been partially asleep and hadn't heard him correctly. Or maybe what Forrest really wanted had unconsciously slipped through his lips. "Why would she be in danger?" Archer wondered aloud.

"I told you about the note," Forrest said.

Maybe he had, but again the chief hadn't been paying much attention yet. He couldn't wake up as quickly as he used to. "Tell me again."

When Forrest did, Archer still wasn't certain how threatening it was. "So somebody was in her house, but he didn't hurt either her or the baby when he'd had the chance?"

"He scared her," Forrest said.

Detective Colton sounded scared, too.

"He threatened her baby," Forrest continued.

"But he didn't hurt him," the chief said. "Of the bodies, we've found none of them was a baby. No baby has been hurt."

"No, it's women who are winding up dead," Forrest said. "So Rae Lemmon's the one in danger."

"We don't have the extra manpower to provide around-the-clock protection for her," Archer said. And he wasn't certain how necessary it was. Sure, someone had been inside her home, but she hadn't been hurt.

If the killer had intended to make her his next victim, he'd had the chance. Now that she'd been warned, she would be more aware, more careful. She didn't need the already limited police resources, and Archer proceeded to tell his new detective this.

"She does," Forrest insisted. "I promised her that she and her son would be protected."

"She can stay with friends or get out of town," Archer suggested, "and she'll be safe."

"No," Forrest said. "The only way she'll be protected is if I do it myself."

Archer cursed. "I need you focused on solving these murders," he reminded him. "That's why I hired you. Not to play bodyguard to a single mom and her infant son."

"I know," Forrest said. "And I'll figure out a way to do both."

Before the chief could say anything else, Colton broke their connection. Not that there was probably anything Archer could have said to change the young detective's mind. Forrest Colton seemed pretty damn determined to play guardian to Rae Lemmon and her baby.

Why?

Was he just concerned about the threat and worried that some harm might actually come to her child or to her? Or was there something else making Forrest Colton so protective?

Was he falling for the single mom?

If that was the case, and that threat was as serious as Forrest believed it was, then she and her baby weren't the only ones in danger. Forrest was in danger, too.

Hell, since the threat was about getting rid of the detective, he was in the most danger—and maybe not just from the person who'd left that note, but from that single mom and her baby, as well.

Chapter 10

He could work anywhere—even in Rae Lemmon's kitchen, even with her wearing just that T-shirt while she slept in her bed just a few yards from where he worked. After his call, he had returned to the nursery to find her already gone.

Which was good because he hadn't wanted to admit to her that the chief hadn't seen the same need for her protection that Forrest had. Was he overreacting?

Not at all.

Somebody had invaded her home. Even if he'd used the key under the flowerpot or found the door unlocked, he had still entered her house without her permission. He had also snipped a piece of hair from Connor's head and left that threatening note.

That was some kind of sick individual to scare a single mom like that. Maybe he was even a killer.

So she and her son absolutely needed protection. Forrest could protect them most if he figured out who the hell had left the note and who had killed those women.

Were they the same person?

He stared down at the pictures he'd spread across her kitchen table. In the light from the pendant hanging over the table, he studied each of the crime-scene photographs for a clue he might have missed, like those buttons had been missed on the first pass through at the drug company's parking lot.

He'd sent those off to the FBI's crime lab because he'd wanted results back faster than he'd been getting them from the Whisperwood crime-scene technicians. But the FBI's lab was backlogged, too. If only solving crimes was as easy as TV shows made it look, then he could have investigated everything and wrapped up all of the cases within an hour.

He'd been staring at these damn pictures for more than sixty minutes, and he hadn't discovered anything new. Hell, he hadn't discovered anything at all. Maybe if Rae wasn't so close…

And so sexy and beautiful that she kept distracting him from his job. But he wasn't even sure what his job was at the moment—to be a detective or a bodyguard.

His physical exhaustion and the weight of his concern for Rae and Connor settled heavily on his shoulders, so heavily that he closed his eyes for a moment. Just a moment…before a soft gasp jerked him fully awake, so awake that he scrambled up and knocked over the chair he'd been using and nearly struck Rae.

She stood next to the table, her brown eyes wide with horror as she stared down at the pictures spread across the white painted surface. "Oh, my."

"I'm sorry," Forrest said. For so many things…

Sorry that he'd let his guard slip long enough for her to sneak up on him.

What if she'd been the intruder?

He was also sorry that she'd seen the gruesome photos of the victims and the crime scenes. With his hands shaking slightly, he swept the pictures back into the folders.

"It's fine," she said despite the catch of emotion in her voice. "I'm going to need to get used to seeing photographs like that with the profession I've chosen."

"Does Lukas, Jolley and Fitzsimmons handle criminal cases?" he asked.

Her eyes went wide again with surprise. "You know where I work?"

He shrugged. "Bellamy must have mentioned it." And he'd paid attention despite himself, because he was so damn curious about Rae Lemmon.

She smiled at his comment. "Bellamy likes to brag about me."

"She does," he agreed. Was that because Rae was her best friend or because she was playing matchmaker?

The same thought might have occurred to Rae, because her face flushed with embarrassment. "To answer your question," she continued, "no, they don't.

But after I pass the bar, I'd like to work in the district attorney's office."

"You want to be a prosecutor?" he asked. Every damn thing she did fascinated him and appealed to him.

She nodded. "Yes. There's been so much crime in Whisperwood lately that I feel compelled to try to help stop some of it."

"That's why you're going to law school while working and raising your son alone?"

She nodded.

"And here I thought you were just a masochist."

She smiled again, and a strange warmth spread throughout his chest. She had a beautiful smile that lit up her chocolate-brown eyes. "That, too," she said, and as if to prove her point, she took the folder from his hand and started flipping through the photographs. The smile left her face, and her eyes darkened with sorrow.

"You don't have to look at those," he said. She probably shouldn't be looking at them, not that she was a potential suspect or anything. But she might know a suspect.

Why else would she have been threatened like she'd been?

"But since you have seen them," he continued, "what are your thoughts? Could these murders have been committed by the same person?"

She shivered even though she wore a light robe over her T-shirt. That must have been for his benefit. But he would have preferred that she'd skipped the robe.

Hell, he would have preferred that she'd skipped

the T-shirt. Heat flushed his face and his body at the thought of seeing her naked, of touching her.

He drew in a deep breath and pushed the image of her, like that, from his mind. He pointed toward the folder. "There was no attempt to mummify the body that was found in the parking lot."

"Maybe he didn't have time," she said. "Maybe he was interrupted. Or not as physically able as he once was."

Forrest sucked in a breath, awed by her insight. "You're going to make a damn good prosecutor."

She smiled and spread that warmth through his chest again. She was so beautiful that he found himself leaning toward her. But before his lips could brush across hers, a cry rent the air between them.

Had someone gotten inside the nursery? Panic replaced the warmth in his chest, pressing heavily against his heart as he ran toward the nursery and Connor.

He would never forgive himself if something happened to the baby because he'd let himself get distracted— because he hadn't been paying close enough attention. And he was pretty damn certain that the baby's mother would never forgive him either.

She would never forgive him for making her fall for him. And she knew she was falling when she watched him once again pick Connor out of his crib and cradle him against his muscular chest. He cuddled her son as if he was the baby's father rather than just his protector.

That was the only reason he was here—to protect them. She had to remind herself of that. But the reminder didn't ease her attraction to him, didn't cool the desire she felt for him, the desire that had kept her from falling back to sleep after she'd left the nursery.

Forrest patted Connor's little bottom. "He's dry," he said. "Why's he crying? Is he hungry?"

She shook her head. "I fed him after you left to make your call." And that had been just a little over an hour ago. Even Connor couldn't be hungry again so soon.

Forrest tensed. "Did you overhear any of that?"

She shook her head. She'd been focused on her son and had also been reluctant to eavesdrop. "Let me take him," she said as she reached out for the baby. Maybe she hadn't burped him well enough before she'd put him back down to sleep.

Forrest had moved his hand from the baby's diapered bottom to his back, and as he patted, Connor spit up all over the front of Forrest's checkered shirt. The detective's hazel eyes widened with shock and horror.

"That's why I wanted him," she said. She hadn't wanted her son to spit up on his protector. "I was afraid that might happen."

Forrest arched a brow over one of his eyes. "You sure you didn't put him up to it?"

Since he'd turned down her invitation to dance, she hadn't been very friendly to him, and her face flushed with embarrassment that he'd stung her pride so much.

"Of course not," she said, but her lips curved into a slight smile. "He's too young to be trained to do stuff like that." Weariness tugged her lips back down. "And if I could train him to do anything, it would be to sleep through the night."

"Don't you know your mama needs her beauty rest?" Forrest asked the baby as he jostled him in his arms.

"Don't—" Rae began. But it was already too late.

The baby threw up even more on Forrest's shirt.

"How much did you feed him?" Forrest asked.

She sighed. "Apparently too much." His bout of colic wasn't helping his digestion any either.

But throwing up must have because his lids began to droop over his big brown eyes, and he nodded back to sleep. She stepped closer and lifted him away from Forrest's chest. "I'll put him down. You can go change your shirt."

"I didn't bring anything to change into," he said. "I didn't realize I was going to wind up staying."

"You didn't have to," she said.

"You wouldn't go to a hotel or your friend's house, so yes, I had to," he said.

He could have left her and Connor alone, to fend for themselves, if the intruder had returned, but he had refused to do that. He was a good man.

After cleaning up a sleeping Connor and settling him back into his crib, she turned toward Forrest, and a gasp slipped through her lips as she discovered that he'd taken off his soiled shirt.

He was a sexy man, too.

So damn sexy…with his heavily muscled chest that was lightly dusted with golden-brown hair.

Her mouth watered, forcing her to swallow down the desire that nearly choked her. She couldn't remember ever wanting anyone the way she wanted Forrest

Colton. What the hell was wrong with her? Was it the lack of sleep? Her fear over the threats?

Or just hormones?

With the shirt dangling from one of his fingers, he asked, "Where's your washing machine?"

Leaving Connor asleep in his crib, she walked on suddenly trembling legs toward the doorway Forrest's big, half-naked body filled. She swallowed again and cleared her throat before replying, "I'll wash it for you." But when she reached for the shirt, he held tightly to it.

"I can do it," he said. "You should go back to sleep."

She doubted that she would be able to sleep now, since she hadn't been able to earlier. Having him in her house had some strange restlessness coursing through her, making her hot and achy in places where she hadn't been hot and achy in a damn long time...if ever.

"Fortunately I function well on small amounts of sleep," she said as she tugged again on the shirt.

"You don't have to," he said.

She smiled. "Just like you didn't have to stay here."

Or change Connor's diaper, or try to comfort him when he was crying...

Damn Forrest Colton. He was definitely making her fall for him. And she knew better than that; she knew he wasn't sticking around Whisperwood. His assignment here was only temporary.

"I have to," he said. "And when I called the chief, he refused to put anyone else on protection duty for you and Connor."

She tensed. "He doesn't think I'm in danger?"

"He doesn't have the resources," Forrest said.

"That's how I got tapped to investigate these cases. Because of Hurricane Brooke, Whisperwood PD is just spread too thin right now."

"And murder investigations would take precedence over the note left on my pillow," she said with a sigh. "You should be working on those cases and not baby-sitting me and my son."

"I promised I would make sure you and Connor stay safe," he said, and his deep hazel eyes filled with intensity as he stared down at her. "And I keep my promises."

She smiled but shook her head. "You won't if you make promises that you can't keep."

"But I—"

She pressed her fingers across his lips before he could finish his protest. "You can't be with us 24/7. You have a job. A life. And so do I. I need to go to work and to my law-school classes."

His lips moved beneath her fingers. "But the threat—"

"Isn't going to stop me from living my life," she said.

"That's exactly what might happen," he pointed out. "If you're not careful."

She smiled again. "I am always very careful." That was why she had used a sperm donor to have a baby—because she was too careful to trust a man to stick around for her and most especially for her child. She didn't want her son to be as disappointed as she had been so often.

"You're not being very careful right now," he murmured, and using their hands on his shirt, he tugged her close, so close that she pressed against his bare chest.

And her breath caught as desire overwhelmed her. His skin was so hot, his body so hard. "Forrest..."

He was right—damn it—because she wasn't being careful. And she was probably going to wind up hurt and disappointed, but she figured she might be even more disappointed if she didn't act on her desire for him.

She would deal with the fallout later.

She dropped his shirt and eased her hands between them, sliding her palms over his bare chest. Soft brown hair covered well-developed muscles that rippled beneath her touch.

He groaned and stumbled back when she pushed him. Then he shook his head and, breathing hard, murmured, "I'm sorry."

She wasn't. Yet.

She pushed him again, out of the nursery, and he stumbled back another step.

"I'll leave you alone," he promised.

"That's not what I want," she said.

"What do you want?" he asked.

"You."

Instead of pushing him, she pulled him now, tugging him toward her bedroom. But he didn't budge, his big body frozen with tension that radiated off him and to her. It gripped her, spiraling inside her with such intensity that she knew she needed to release it. If she didn't, she might explode into a million pieces.

"Are you sure?" he asked, his voice gruff with passion and something else.

Something like vulnerability.

Clearly Bellamy and Maggie had been right; his fiancée had done a number on him when she'd taken off like she had—the same number Rae's deadbeat dad had done on her.

"I'm sure," she said, and to convince him, she rose on tiptoe and pressed her lips to his.

His arms closed around her, holding her against him as he kissed her back. But then he pulled away and murmured, "This is a mistake."

And she tensed. "I'm sorry." Tears stung her eyes; this time his rejection hurt more than just her pride. "I need to stop throwing myself at you."

He chuckled, a deep chuckle that rumbled in his naked chest. "You're not throwing yourself." His chuckle turned to a groan. "But even if you had, I would catch you and not let you go." His arms tightened around her.

She pulled back, staring up at his handsome face. His jaw was so tightly clenched, a muscle pulsated in his cheek. "I thought it was a mistake."

"It is," he said. "I need to stay focused on protecting you. But I want to do so much more."

Her breath escaped in a gasp of relief. He wasn't rejecting her. "We're safe," she said. "Nobody has tried to get inside." And she doubted that they would with his police vehicle parked outside. "Nobody's out there."

"I hope you're right," he said, and he lowered his head and kissed her again.

He was out there—watching the shadows behind the curtains, watching as they moved together toward that front bedroom.

She hadn't heeded his threat. Hell, it wasn't his

threat. It was the threat of a killer—a killer who wanted this detective off the murder cases so badly that he would do anything.

Even kill again.

The baby? Or him?

If he didn't get the detective to back off, would he, despite trying to get rid of the lawman, be the next victim? It was a chance he couldn't take—even if he wound up becoming a killer himself.

Chapter 11

The law office of Lukas, Jolley and Fitzsimmons wasn't far from the Whisperwood Police Department. Forrest wanted to continue driving past the brick building without letting out Rae or Connor, but she reached across the console of her SUV and gripped his knee.

His entire body reacted just as it had last night. Tension filled him, and his erection throbbed behind the fly of his wrinkled dress pants.

"This is it," she said. "Where I work."

"You shouldn't be going to work," he said. "It's too dangerous."

But it would have been more dangerous had they stayed inside her house together because they would have given in to the attraction between them, just as they had the night before. Or had that really happened?

Or had he only dreamed it?

He had been so exhausted that he might have nodded off at the table and only imagined they'd made love. But he hadn't awakened at the table; he'd awakened in her bed, with her naked body clasped in his arms, and her head nestled between his neck and shoulder.

How had he been so irresponsible? So reckless? The intruder could have returned when they'd been making love or when they'd fallen asleep.

Forrest had rushed out of bed then to check on Connor, to make sure nothing had happened to him. The baby had been fine. But Forrest was not.

He would never be fine again. What had happened between them…

Rae tightened her grip on his thigh. "Forrest, please."

She'd said that last night, when he'd kissed his way from her lips down her entire body. She'd begged for more. But she hadn't been the only one.

He had worried that he might not survive the onslaught of emotion when she'd returned his favor and kissed him all over, including the scars on his wounded leg. Shannon had been so horrified of his injury that she'd run away. But Rae…

Rae was different. She'd stuck around after her father had taken off and had cared for her sick mother. Rae was caring and compassionate.

And passionate and…

"Forrest," she said again.

With a sigh of resignation, he turned around in a parking lot a block past the law building and headed back to her work. Finally she moved her hand from his leg, and he sighed again, but with regret. Despite the tension it caused, he wanted her touching him—like she'd touched him last night.

But she'd turned around to peer into the back seat, where the baby carrier was secured. "We should have dropped off Connor first."

"You're sure he will be safe at the day care?" Forrest asked as he had the first time.

She smiled. "Yes, there's no way Bob McCauley would let anything happen to him."

"Bob McCauley?" The name sounded vaguely familiar to him but not as a day care owner. "Didn't he play professional football?"

She smiled. "Yes, he did. So you know that nobody would try anything with Bob protecting Connor."

Even though Forrest recognized the name, he didn't know the man, so he wanted to talk to him before determining if he trusted Connor in his care. Rae hadn't wanted to be late for work, though, so she'd asked to be dropped off first. He also wanted to make sure she would be safe before he left her, so he parked her SUV and insisted on following her up to her office, while carrying the handle of the carrier with the sleeping baby over his arm.

An odd chill swept over him, despite the heat of the Texas sun bearing down on them already. He glanced around the lot, looking for someone watching them, and his free hand moved toward his holster. Had someone followed them from the house? Or had the person been waiting here, at her work, for Rae's arrival?

The morning sun glinting off all of the vehicles'

tinted windows made it impossible to see inside, to see if anyone was inside, watching them. But that sensation prickling Forrest's skin and raising the short hairs on the nape of his neck confirmed to him that someone was there.

Maybe not the person who'd left the threat for Rae, but someone.

He tightened his grip on the baby carrier and stepped closer to her. Rae's body tensed as he did. Did she feel it, too? Had last night affected her like it had him?

She'd been acting all morning like it hadn't happened, though.

Maybe that was why he kept wondering if he'd only dreamed it—because he seemed to be the only one who remembered it. Or wanted to remember it.

She hastened her step as if trying to create some distance between them. But he lengthened his stride and, despite his limp, managed to keep close—for her protection. But she didn't look as if she felt safe.

Hell, she wouldn't look at him at all. She pushed open the door to the foyer and rushed toward the bank of elevators. When the doors to one of the elevator cars opened, she stepped inside and hurriedly pressed a button as if she was trying to escape him. He—and Connor—joined her before the doors closed. Despite already pushing the button for her floor, she kept staring at the panel as if she preferred looking at it to looking at him.

Since they'd awakened that morning, she really hadn't looked at him, as if she couldn't bear to face him. Or face what they'd done?

Did she regret making love with him? Had it only been a moment of weakness—of vulnerability—for her?

Guilt settled heavily onto his shoulders that he'd taken advantage of that vulnerability, of her fear. Sure, she'd insisted that wasn't the case, that she'd really wanted him.

And that had seemed true with the way she'd touched him, the way she'd kissed him, the way she'd cried out with pleasure when she...

Now heat rushed to his face and suffused the rest of his body. He drew in a shaky breath to settle himself, to control the urge for him to lean closer to her and press his lips to hers. To remind her of the heat of the desire between them, the passion.

As he began to bend toward her, though, the elevator lurched to a stop and the bell dinged. The doors slid open, and she stepped out of the car. Only then did she turn back to face him. "You don't have to come any farther," she told him. "I'm on my floor. I'm safe."

As if the matter was settled, she crouched down to peer into the carrier at her baby. "Be good," she told the sleeping infant.

Love glowed on her beautiful face, warming her brown eyes. She loved her son so much that it radiated from her. Then she lifted her gaze to Forrest and the warmth left her eyes as her guard went back up. "Please make sure he gets safely to day care."

"I will," he promised. "I'll protect him." Or die trying.

Her lips tugged down at the corners. "I warned you about making promises you can't keep."

"I will keep this one," he vowed. "I will."

She sighed and stepped back, and the doors began to close. A sense of panic rushed over him, and he slapped his hand against them, holding them open. "I should make sure you're safe here," he said.

Her smile flashed. "I am fine. I can take care of myself."

She was Bellamy's age—thirty-five—so she'd been taking care of herself for a while now. So he believed her.

That didn't make him feel any better, though. Somehow it made him feel worse—like he had personally put her in danger. But all he'd done was find that body in her backyard; someone else had put it there.

Someone she knew?

She pushed his hand back from the door, and his skin tingled even from that slight contact. "Take Connor to day care and get back to your real job," she told him. "You don't need to babysit either of us now."

She lifted the hand that had touched his to her lips and pressed a kiss to it. And his heart caught when she blew that kiss…until he realized she was blowing it at her son. Not at him.

After she blew it, she turned on the wedge heel of her sandal and started down the hallway. A man stood in an open doorway to one of the offices, staring at her. Forrest could understand why he stared. She looked beautiful in a yellow dress that clung to her shapely curves and sleek legs.

Something tightened in his chest, like someone was squeezing his heart. While he understood it, he didn't like how that man looked at her. And he wondered how she would look at him. The doors closed before he could witness their interaction, but it left him wondering.

What kind of threat had that note been?

A serious one?

Or one designed to manipulate her into reaching out to help from a friend? Or someone who wanted to be more than a friend?

Forrest couldn't be certain, though, if it was his detective instincts that had come up with that possibility or his jealousy. Despite what had happened between them last night, he had no right to feel jealous or possessive of Rae Lemmon. Hell, he'd never felt jealous over anyone before—not even his fiancée.

No. He was probably just concerned—because when he left he had that feeling again, like someone was watching him. Was it the person who'd threatened Rae or someone else?

Once Rae turned away from the elevator, a sudden panic struck her, stealing her breath away and making her knees tremble. She turned back, but the doors had already closed. And the button above them showed that it was descending, taking her son and Forrest away from her.

Just for the workday.

They would come back for her. Forrest had promised that he would keep Connor safe. That he would protect her son.

She really didn't want him making her any promises,

though. Her father had made her more than enough of those, promises that Beau Lemmon had never managed to keep. Had he even intended to when he'd made them?

Rae doubted it. He'd probably only been telling her what she'd wanted to hear, that he would come back.

That he would get his act together so that he could be the husband her mother deserved and the father she deserved. But that was a promise he had never kept.

Forrest clearly intended to keep his promise, to keep her and Connor safe. But she didn't know if that was a promise he would be able to keep or if the person who'd left that threat was more determined than he was.

"Who was that?" someone asked.

Rae turned back to find Kenneth Dawson standing in the open door to his office. She forced a smile. "Just a friend."

But images of the night before, of how Forrest had kissed her, touched her, pleasured her…rushed through her mind. Her pulse quickened, and her flesh heated—just as it had the night before. She'd never experienced anything as powerful as making love with Forrest. Last night had been amazing. Forrest Colton had been amazing.

His fiancée had been an idiot to leave a man like that. His injured leg hadn't hindered him at all—in the bedroom or in life. In fact, it had probably only made him stronger and more resolved.

So when he made a promise, he would do everything he could to keep it. But would it be enough?

"Must be a good friend for you to trust him with your baby," Kenneth murmured. "Or is he the father?"

Rae wished that Connor had a man like that in his life for more than protection. But she would be enough for her son. Just like her mother had been enough—more than enough—for her.

"Rae?" Kenneth prodded her. "Is he?"

She turned back toward the man, and as she drew in a deep breath, she reminded herself that he was one of her superiors at the firm, even though his name wasn't technically on the sign. She could not reply as she wanted—to tell him to mind his own damn business. Forcing a smile, she shook her head. "No. He isn't. That was Detective Colton with the Whisperwood Police Department."

"He's the one who found the body in your backyard," he said.

She wasn't certain how he would know that unless the media had mentioned it. But in every news report she had seen, Forrest or the chief had refused to answer questions about an ongoing investigation.

As if he'd noticed her suspicion, he reminded her, "I heard it on the police scanner."

She suppressed a little shiver of revulsion over his being such an ambulance chaser. It was lawyers like Kenneth Dawson who had earned the profession the bad reputation.

That was why she wanted to work on the other side—for the prosecution. For law and order, and not financial gain.

But Kenneth had always been nice to her, so she

forced another smile for him. "That's right. Well, I better get to my desk. I'm sure I have a lot of work to do."

He stepped out of his doorway just as she headed toward her office, and she accidentally brushed up against him when she passed. Another shiver of revulsion coursed through her. Wasn't he the nice man she'd wanted to believe he was?

Or maybe it was just that damn note that was making her suspicious of everyone. Except Forrest.

She knew that he would do his best to protect her and Connor—even though the chief hadn't taken the threat as seriously as he had.

Forrest had done more than protect them last night, though. He'd made her feel things she hadn't felt in so long—if ever. So much damn pleasure that it had overwhelmed her.

Even thinking about it now overwhelmed her. The way he'd kissed her, touched her, moved inside her...

Heat coursed through her body now as she remembered how he'd made her feel. Her hand shook as she turned the knob on her door and pushed it open. Her legs trembled as she crossed the threshold and headed toward her desk.

Forrest was such a thorough lover. He'd made certain that she'd found her pleasure—many times—before he'd taken his own. She'd never known so generous a man. Most of them she'd known had been selfish.

Could she really trust that Forrest was that different, that he might actually stick around? She doubted it. His only interest in her was protecting her and Connor. Well, maybe not his only interest.

But she couldn't give in to that desire again. She would only fall for him more deeply than she had already.

She dropped into the chair behind her desk and reached for the mail the clerk had left on the corner of it. She handled a lot of the incoming correspondence. So she began rifling through it. One of the envelopes bore only her name, though. No address. Nothing to do with the law firm at all.

Who would have sent something to her at the office?

It must have been an interoffice message from one of the partners. Maybe from Kenneth, although he usually liked to come and talk to her personally.

She sliced the envelope open and dumped out a single folded sheet of paper. When she unfolded the note, she found the same scrawled block letters that she'd found on the slip of paper on her pillow. The message was a little different, though.

It was more threatening.

Get rid of the detective, or your kid won't be the only one who suffers.

"Oh, my God," she murmured. She needed to call Forrest to warn him. Somebody really wanted him gone, so much so that they were willing to hurt a baby and her to get to him. She fumbled her cell phone out of her purse and punched in the contact Bellamy had given her for Forrest.

"This is Forrest Colton, interim detective with the Whisperwood Police Department, please leave a message and I'll return your call."

Why had it gone directly to voice mail?

Why wasn't he picking up?

She left a message. "Call me back. I just got another threat."

But would he be able to return her call?

Or had she tried to warn him too late?

The cell phone sitting on the table at JoJo's Java began to vibrate, and the screen lit up with a number Jonah Colton didn't recognize. His beautiful fiancée leaned across the table between them, her blond hair sliding across her cheek as she glanced down at the screen.

"Probably a telemarketer," he commented as he left the phone lying there. He would rather focus on Maggie than an offer for new windows, cable or a way to reduce his nonexistent credit-card debt.

She shook her head, though, so she must have recognized the number. "You need to get that. It's Rae."

Jonah furrowed his brow. "Why would she be calling me?" Maggie had filled him in on what had happened to her friend—about the threatening note and that Rae had called Forrest to report it.

Forrest would have handled the threat. Despite his injured leg, he was every bit the outstanding lawman he'd always been. It was too damn bad that, because he hadn't been able to meet the physical requirements of his job, Austin PD had forced him to retire on disability. That limp didn't slow down Forrest at all.

So, why would Rae be calling Jonah?

Had something happened?

He grabbed up the phone and hit the accept button. "Rae, is everything all right?"

"No," she said, her voice tremulous with fear. "I don't know what Maggie told you—"

"Everything," he interjected. He and his fiancée had no secrets. Only love and understanding.

Her shaky breath of relief rattled his phone. "I got another threat—at the office—about Connor and Forrest," she said.

"Did you show it to Forrest?"

"He left with Connor," she said, and her voice cracked again. "And he's not picking up his phone."

Her fear filled him now, and he jumped up from his chair. "I'll find him," he said.

"Hurry," Rae implored him. "This threat was left in my office."

According to Maggie, the other one had been left on a pillow on her bed. The person threatening her had to be someone close to her.

Rae had apparently come to the same conclusion, because she added, "If he knows where I work and where I live, he probably knows where Connor's day care is. Forrest was going there with my son when he left me at the office."

And now she couldn't reach him.

She had to be terrified about her child. "Please find them," she pleaded.

It was clear that Connor wasn't the only one she was worried about; she was worried about Forrest, as well.

So was Jonah. "What day care?" he asked.

"I know," Maggie said. She'd jumped up from her chair as well, forgetting her coffee. "I'll go with you."

He shook his head. If Forrest was in danger, and it certainly sounded as if he was, then Jonah had no intention of putting his fiancée in danger, too.

But she headed out the door ahead of him, straight for their vehicle. From the urgency in Rae's voice, he didn't have time to fight with Maggie. So he just hurried after her. "I'll let you know when I find them," he told Rae before clicking off his cell.

He only hoped when he had found them that he would have good news to share with her. As one of the Cowboy Heroes, unfortunately he usually had more bad news to share than good.

Chapter 12

He hadn't been wrong. Someone had been watching him and Rae arrive at her office. Fortunately that someone had followed him from the lot instead of staying behind to stalk Rae.

But then again the threat had been against her child—not her—and Connor slept peacefully in the back seat. Peacefully but not exactly safely, not with the big cargo van following them. The van windows were tinted, so Forrest couldn't see the driver or even how many passengers might be inside with him. Was Forrest outnumbered?

He reached for his cell, but when he pulled it from his pocket, the screen was black. He hadn't brought a charger to Rae's last night, and the battery must have died. A curse slipped through his lips, followed by a twinge of guilt striking his heart. He glanced back at Connor, but the baby was still asleep. Even if he hadn't been, though, he probably wouldn't have understood what Forrest had said, and he certainly couldn't repeat it. Yet.

Forrest had to make sure that Connor would have the chance someday to talk, to curse, to grow up.

He had to make sure he kept his promise to Rae and kept her son safe. The van edged closer, as if the driver was no longer worried about Forrest's noticing him.

Another curse burned his throat, but he forced it down. Swearing wasn't going to help him, and with his dead phone, he couldn't call for backup. He had to protect Connor himself.

As he pressed down on the accelerator, he glanced into the rearview mirror. He wasn't looking at the van behind him, though. He was trying to see the car seat, to make sure he'd secured it like Rae had showed him. She'd been adamant about how to install it so that the baby would be safe.

But he'd removed it at her office and had then put it back in without her supervision. Had he done it right?

Would Connor be safe at this speed?

He glanced up from the baby to the back window, where he saw the van was now so close that its grille was all Forrest saw. He pressed on the accelerator again just as the van brushed the back bumper of Rae's small SUV. Then he jerked the wheel and took a sudden turn onto a side street. The van passed it, but the brakes squealed as it stopped and backed up.

The driver was determined. But so was Forrest. He'd

grown up in Whisperwood; he knew all of the streets well. Using his knowledge, he led the van around the city. But the driver must have known the city well, too, because Forrest didn't lose his tail.

The van also had a more powerful engine, because it easily kept up with the speeding SUV. Where were the police officers? Why had nobody stopped them?

But that was why Forrest had been hired, despite his disability, because the department was spread so thin—too thin obviously to patrol the streets. Too bad the day care had been in the opposite direction from the police department, or he would have been closer to Whisperwood PD.

He headed there now, though, but the driver sped up. If he knew Whisperwood as well as he seemed to, he might have guessed where Forrest was heading. And he was determined that he and Connor would not make it there.

The driver closed the distance between the vehicles and struck the back of the SUV hard. Connor awoke with a scream. Forrest cursed as he gripped the wheel, struggling not to lose control.

But the van struck again and again.

And Forrest worried that Rae had been right not to trust him. He shouldn't have made the promise to her— because he wasn't going to be able to keep it after all.

Rae had expected a call back. She'd hoped for a quick assurance from Forrest that he and Connor were all right, that he'd just been too busy talking to Bob McCauley to answer his phone.

But she knew that if he'd been able, Forrest would have taken her call. He wouldn't have wanted to worry her, and he would have been worried about her. She didn't take that personally, though, even after last night. He was just doing his job. He wasn't just a detective; he was a lawman who'd sworn years ago to serve and protect. And he'd promised to protect them, as if the threat was somehow his fault.

But he'd only been doing his job when she'd received that threat. A job that someone obviously didn't want him doing. It had to be the killer leaving the notes. Who else would want to get rid of Forrest?

She'd once thought she had when he'd showed up at her back door that day he'd found the body. Now she didn't want him gone. She just wanted him to be all right.

He and Connor had to be okay.

He'd promised.

The phone call she wanted never came. Instead Jonah Colton showed up in her office doorway. She'd been staring at it since she'd called him. But his wasn't the face she'd wanted to see looking in at her.

And even if she had, she wouldn't have wanted to see him like this—his jaw tense, his face pale with concern or fear. Heart pounding, she jumped up from her chair. "What is it? What's wrong?"

She peered around him, looking for Forrest. Maybe he'd just moved slower due to his limp; maybe that was why he wasn't in the doorway, too. But she knew—she just knew—there was another reason.

"There's been an accident," Jonah said, confirming her fears.

"Accident?" She shook her head in denial. "It was no accident." She reached back and grabbed her purse from her desk. Then she shoved past him in the doorway. "Where are they? Where are Connor and Forrest?"

"At the hospital," he replied, his voice soft with sympathy and that concern that pinched his handsome face.

Panic nearly buckled her knees, making her stumble as she headed toward the elevator. Jonah reached out and steadied her with his hand on her elbow.

"I'll bring you there," he said.

Her son was in the hospital. He was so little, so fragile…

What the hell had happened?

She wanted to know the details about that, but more important she wanted to know that he was all right. She had to make sure that he was all right.

Jonah pushed the button for the elevator, and the doors immediately opened. They stepped inside, and he pushed the button for the lobby. He was in as much of a rush to get her to the hospital as she was. If he hadn't offered to drive her, she would have run to the hospital. Nothing and nobody would keep her from her child.

And Forrest.

Her stomach pitched as the elevator stopped in the lobby. What had happened to him?

Tears stung her eyes as fear overwhelmed her. If only she had listened to him and hadn't gone to work.

He could have kept her and Connor safe at their

home, as he had last night. But Forrest hadn't just kept them safe; he'd made love to Rae and had made her start to fall in love with him.

If something had happened to him…

If something had happened to either of them…

She would personally track down the person who'd hurt them. And that person would pay for what he'd done.

"You're going to pay up one way or the other," his caller said.

He didn't recognize the voice emanating from the phone any more than he had recognized the handwriting on the notes that had been left in his motel room for him. But he didn't have to know who his caller was to know what he was: a killer.

And now he might be the same. Regret and self-disgust churned his stomach, making bile rise up in his throat.

"So you damn well better have done what I ordered," his new boss continued.

"I did," he said. "I did what you wanted."

"You got rid of the detective from Austin?"

"Yeah…" And probably not just him.

A memory ran through his mind, of Colton carrying the baby seat through the parking lot at the law office. Of him securing it into the back seat of Rae's SUV.

How secure had it been?

"You damn well better have," the person continued, his voice gruff with disgust. "You owe me a hell of a lot of money."

He flinched. That wasn't the way it had started out,

or the way it should have wound up. But nothing in his life had ever wound up the way he had expected it to.

Not his career.

Or his family.

Not one damn thing about his life.

His luck had run out a long time ago. He was the only one who hadn't realized it, though. Everybody else had just kept collecting IOUs from him—until his debt had become insurmountable.

What about Forrest Colton? How lucky was he? Had he survived the crash?

If the detective had survived this attempt, he would not be able to survive the next. Or *he* was going to wind up repaying his debt with his own life.

Chapter 13

Fury coursed through Forrest. "I don't care that I'm not the baby's legal guardian," he said. "I want to know how Connor is doing."

The nurse at the desk remained stone-faced as she just shook her head in reply to his questions. He'd been able to crack hardened criminals easier than this woman.

"You need to return to the examination area, Mr. Colton," she said, "while we're awaiting the results of your CAT scan."

He touched his forehead. "It's just a bump." That throbbed like hell, but he knew enough to know it wasn't serious. Neither was the pain reverberating from his hip down his leg. That was because of the seat belt and the bump on his knee that matched the one on his head.

Because of a faulty airbag, the dashboard had done more damage to him than the crash had. But he didn't give a damn about his own injuries.

"I am responsible for that baby," Forrest said.

"I thought you admitted you're not the father," the nurse reminded him, her brow furrowed as she studied his face.

Forrest cursed his own damn honesty, wishing he'd lied now. At least then they would have let him be with Connor. Had they allowed Maggie back to see him?

"I am a detective with the Whisperwood Police Department," Forrest said, and he pulled out his temporary badge to show her. "I am responsible for Connor Lemmon because I was protecting him."

But he hadn't done a very damn good job. He hadn't been able to outrun the van, which had kept ramming into them until the SUV had crashed into a parked car.

Forrest didn't know what had happened next. He might have blacked out for a couple of seconds— because the van was gone when he opened his eyes. And Connor had been screaming hysterically.

Forrest had forced open the crumpled door of the SUV, but when he'd stepped out, he'd nearly collapsed on the street from the pain radiating throughout his bad leg. Even now it threatened to buckle, so he leaned more heavily on the edge of the nurses' station.

"I need to know how he is," he persisted. He needed to know how badly he'd broken his promise to Rae.

The baby had looked fine when Forrest had forced open the back door and unclasped his carrier from the seat. The harness seemed to have held him mostly immobile.

But babies were fragile.

The little guy could have had internal injuries, wounds that Forrest hadn't been able to see. Fortunately someone had witnessed the crash and called 911, so an ambulance, with sirens blaring, had roared up at the same time Jonah and Maggie had. They'd followed the ambulance, with him and Connor inside, to the hospital. But once in the ER, he and the infant had been separated for treatment.

He'd thought he would be able to see Connor again, but the damn staff had refused to reunite them. Why?

"What's wrong with him?" he asked the nurse. Maybe that was why she wouldn't tell him, because it was so bad. Panic gripped him as he considered how bad it could be.

Fatal.

Rae had already suffered so many losses: her father's abandonment during her mother's illness, and then her mother's death. But losing her son...

How would someone ever recover from that?

Forrest had known the infant for only a few days, and he was in pain—a pain that was so much more debilitating than physical injuries. His heart ached with it.

"Mr. Colton," the nurse said as she came out from behind the desk.

He turned toward her, and as he loosened his grip on the counter, his leg shook beneath him, nearly dropping him to the floor.

"You need to return to the examination table," she said. "You probably have a concussion, and your leg—"

"It's a mess," he finished for her. "It's been a mess since I was shot. I don't have any injuries from the crash." None that compared to the gunshot wound that had shattered bone and left him permanently disabled. "What I do have is a responsibility to the person I was protecting and a right to know how he's doing."

She uttered a weary-sounding sigh. "You are persistent."

Not persistent enough to have kept his promise to Rae, though.

"Return to your examination area at least until we get back the results of your CAT scan, and I'll—" she lowered her voice and whispered "—tell you about the baby."

A moment of panic struck him. Now that she'd agreed to share Connor's condition with him, Forrest wasn't sure he wanted to know.

What if he'd broken his promise?

What if he'd failed Rae?

She would never forgive him.

And neither would Forrest ever forgive himself.

Rae clasped Connor's limp body to her madly pounding heart. He seemed so lifeless, but for the soft breaths escaping his lips. He was alive.

Tears of relief coursed down her face.

"He's fine," Maggie assured her. "The doctor just told us that he has no injuries—no effects—from the accident at all."

Rae had heard him, too. But she hadn't believed it until she'd held Connor, until she'd felt his warmth and heard the sounds of his soft breathing.

"He must just be exhausted," Maggie said as she stared at the baby, too. Her beautiful blue eyes were damp with either tears of relief or of the fear she'd felt when she'd realized that he'd been in an accident.

Rae nodded in agreement with Maggie's assessment. Connor got like this—limp with exhaustion—after he cried, and she imagined he must have been crying during and after the crash. That he must have been terrified.

"What happened?" she asked. Now that she knew he was all right, she wanted those details. But before giving Maggie a chance to answer, she added, "How is Forrest?"

"Sorry," a deep voice said, and then the curtain around Connor's examination area was pulled aside to reveal Forrest. A red bump swelled on his forehead, and he leaned on one crutch for support.

A twinge of pain struck her heart over his injuries. He had not escaped as unscathed as Connor had. "Are you okay?" she asked.

He nodded. "I'm fine." He didn't look fine. His jaw was clenched and his hazel eyes were dark with concern. He gestured at Connor. "How is he?"

More tears welled in her eyes—more tears of relief— that Forrest had survived, as well. Emotion choked her, and she couldn't speak for a moment.

Maggie answered for her. "He's really fine. Not even a bump or a bruise—unlike you."

"That nurse wouldn't give me any information about Connor's condition, but she told you about mine?" Forrest asked.

Maggie pointed at his head. "She didn't need to say anything. It's clear you didn't escape without any injuries like Connor did."

A ragged breath of relief escaped his lips. "He's really okay?" He wasn't looking at Maggie, though. He was looking at Rae.

She nodded. "Yes, he is."

"I'm sorry," he said again. "I had a feeling there was someone in the parking lot of the law office. And then he started following us to the day care center."

He hadn't just followed them, though.

"I tried to lose him," Forrest said.

"Him?" Rae asked. "You saw him?"

He shook his head. "The windows were tinted, so I couldn't see who was behind the wheel. And after he forced us off the road, he drove off. He got away."

She shivered and clutched Connor tighter in her arms. He had gotten away, so he could come back. To her house. To her office. Here.

She shuddered. "We need to get Connor out of here," she said.

As if he'd read her mind, Forrest assured her, "He's safe. This place has some pretty tough security, and that's just the nurses."

One of them had followed him inside the curtained area, and she glared at him now. "Mr. Colton was quite concerned about your son," she told Rae. Then she turned back toward him. "But you can see that he's fine. You, on the other hand…"

"What?" Rae asked. "Isn't he okay?"

The nurse ignored her as she continued to speak to Forrest. "We got back the results of the X-rays on your leg and the CAT scan on your head."

"And I'm fine," Forrest insisted.

But the nurse didn't confirm this. All she said was, "You need to speak to the doctor, Mr. Colton."

And the crushing panic returned to Rae's chest, pressing down on her lungs and heart so that she had to struggle to breathe. "Forrest…"

But the nurse was already leading him away from her.

Maggie stepped closer and wrapped her arm around Rae's waist. "I'm sure he's fine," she said.

"Then why wouldn't she tell him that?"

Maggie shrugged. "Privacy rules. She wouldn't give us any information about Connor until you got here, and then the doctor had to do it."

Rae nodded in agreement. "That's right. That has to be what it is."

But would Forrest's results be as good as Connor's?

With the bump on his head and the crutch under his arm, he had obvious injuries. How severe were they? And were there any other ones?

Concussion? Broken bones? Internal injuries?

He'd promised to protect them, but at what cost to himself? His life?

Josephine Colton studied her husband's face as he held his phone to his ear, listening. The color had left his skin, and there was a slight tremble along his jaw. "You'll let us know how he is and if we need to come."

It wasn't a question. He was informing his caller that it was required. While always diplomatic and polite, her husband had a backbone of steel, and anyone who'd worked for him or that he'd raised would attest to it. The steel was bending a bit with age and worry over those kids they'd raised.

The minute he clicked off his cell, she asked, "Who is it?"

But there was a part of her that knew already. The minute he'd accepted the interim position with the Whisperwood Police Department, she'd begun to worry that this would happen again, that he would be wounded in the line of duty.

Hays had worried, too. And he was worried now, with deep grooves beside his mouth and between his brows. "Forrest."

Her fears confirmed, she gasped. "How badly?"

"According to Jonah, he's conscious and pissed off," Hays replied with a smile he mustered for her sake.

She smiled back at him, like he wanted her to, but her fears did not subside. He'd been conscious and pissed off after he'd been shot in the leg, and that injury had been so severe, the doctors had thought they might have to amputate.

"What happened?" she asked.

He shook his head. "Something to do with Bellamy and Maggie's friend Rae."

The pretty brunette. Josephine had seen her talk to

Forrest at the wedding, but he'd walked away from her then. "Is she all right?"

"She wasn't in the car with him," Hays replied, and his brow furrowed more as he added, "but her baby was."

Josephine gasped again with fear for the infant. He was so young, so fragile. "Is he all right?"

Hays shook his head. "I don't know."

"We should go to the hospital." She glanced around the farmhouse kitchen. Where had she put her purse? Hell, she didn't need it. She just needed to make sure her son was all right and that Rae Lemmon's son was, too.

"Jonah said he would call back once he knew more," Hays said, and he walked over and put his arm around her. "You know how tough Forrest is. By the time we'd get there, I'm sure he would have already checked himself out."

"With or against doctor's orders," she murmured. Because he was that stubborn.

And that stubbornness would probably be the death of him. Or of her.

Josephine loved all of her boys, but she didn't love worrying about them like she did. And since they'd all chosen to be lawmen or military men or rescuers, she was constantly worrying about their physical and emotional well-being.

Dallas was still devastated from losing his wife, and Forrest over losing his job. Only Donovan and Jonah were truly happy now. She wanted that kind of happiness for all of her children.

Chapter 14

The front door closed behind Jonah and Maggie, leaving Forrest and Rae alone in the living room. Connor, exhausted from the ordeal, slept peacefully now in his crib. Forrest and Jonah had searched the house the minute they'd arrived, looking for any more notes or signs of another intrusion.

But they had found nothing here.

"I have an officer picking up the note from your office, along with all of the building's security footage from the morning," Forrest said. "Hopefully we'll be able to figure out who left that note on your desk."

They already knew why. Someone wanted him out of the way.

Either because of the investigation or because of her.

That was why Forrest had returned to her house

when he'd really wanted to assign the young officer to protection duty instead. He hadn't talked to the chief yet, but surely the guy had to see that Rae was in real danger. Or at least her son was, and who wouldn't deem security necessary for a defenseless infant?

Forrest sucked in a breath as he relived those interminable moments when he hadn't known how Connor was, if he'd survived the crash without injury.

And he remembered that he needed to call his folks. Unfortunately Jonah had told them what had happened, and they were worried. Now he understood some of what they must be feeling.

Not that Connor was his kid. But he cared about the little guy. And he cared about Rae. Too much.

Too much to stick around if it was his presence that was putting them in danger. But was the reason someone wanted him gone more to do with Rae than the murder investigation?

Did she have some admirer or stalker who wanted her all to himself?

Another memory flitted through his head of that lawyer watching Rae from his doorway. The way he'd looked at her…

It hadn't been like a boss should look at an employee, or a colleague at a coworker. It had been how a man looks at a woman he wants.

The way Forrest looked at Rae.

He wanted her.

Maybe that was the real reason he'd come back to the house with her instead of assigning that young officer. Not that he intended to be as selfish as he had been the night before.

He couldn't act on his desire for her. He couldn't risk being distracted, not after someone had tried and nearly succeeded to kill him and Connor.

"You're right," she said.

He tensed. Had she read his mind? Did she know what he'd been thinking—about what they'd done the night before, about what he wanted to do to her now?

"It's too dangerous for me to go to the office, to bring Connor to day care," she said, and she shivered. Wrapping her arms around herself for warmth or comfort, she added, "I don't want to think about what might have happened if you and Connor had made it to the day care, if something happened to him there or to the other children." She shivered again.

His chest ached with the need to wrap his arms around her, to comfort her. But he knew that his comforting her might lead to more, like it had the night before.

"I'm sorry," she continued. "I should have listened to you." She stepped closer then, and after unwrapping her arms from around herself, she reached for him.

But he stumbled back a step, to avoid her touch.

She flinched and murmured again, "I'm sorry. I'm sorry you got hurt."

"I'm fine," he said.

She narrowed her eyes and studied his face with suspicion. "The ER doctor seemed concerned about you leaving the hospital."

He shrugged. "He was worried that I might have a slight concussion." He touched the bump on his head and winced. "Because of this. But my head is hard as a rock." The gnawing ache in his leg that radiated out from the bump on his knee to his ankle and up to his hip bothered him more. But he'd refused to take any painkillers for it.

He needed to stay sharp in order to find out who the hell was threatening her and her son. And because he needed to stay sharp, he needed to fight his attraction to her. But she looked so beautiful in that sunny yellow dress that skimmed over her curves.

"What about your leg?" she asked, and her gaze ran down his body.

His traitorous body hardened in reaction to just that look, and it was one of concern, not desire. But then she sucked in a breath as if she'd noticed how the fly of pants was strained now.

"My leg is fine, too," he said, and it was, since that ache had moved to another part of his body. He turned away from her and peered through the nursery doorway.

"Did I hear something?" he asked despite the silence. Connor needed to wake up so that Forrest would come to his senses, so that he wouldn't be tempted to act on his attraction again.

Rae glanced toward the outside door instead, and her brown eyes widened with fear. "Did you? Do you think someone's out there?"

He stifled a groan. "No," he assured her.

But could he be certain?

He didn't necessarily think the person who'd threatened them was out there, but he wondered about Jonah. Had his brother really left?

Forrest wouldn't have put it past him to stick around. Ever since he'd been shot, his brothers had been extra concerned about him. So had his parents.

He needed to check in with them as Jonah had suggested, to make sure that they weren't too upset. He was upset enough for all of them. But he wasn't concerned about his life; he was worried about hers and about Connor's.

If he was worried at all about himself, it wasn't about his life but about his heart. He'd had it broken too recently for him to trust it with anyone else yet. Even Rae.

Maybe most especially Rae, who had already declared her determination to raise her son alone. She wasn't looking for any man, least of all a disabled one who had already put her new family in danger.

"I'm the one who's sorry," he said. "I'm the reason you started getting those threats." And by sticking around, he wasn't necessarily protecting her and Connor but was probably putting them in more danger. "I'm the one this person wants gone."

Yet here he was. He'd insisted that Jonah bring them all back to her house.

"So maybe I should leave," he suggested.

She shuddered. "Whoever he is, he doesn't want you just to go away. He wants you dead. He tried to kill you today."

"And Connor could have been hurt in the cross fire," Forrest said, guilt churning his stomach into knots. If anything had happened to her baby, he never would have forgiven himself. And neither would she have.

"That's why I should go," he continued. "And why I should stay away from you."

For Connor's sake, for hers and for his, too.

He couldn't risk his heart again—not even for Rae. Not that she probably wanted him to. All she'd wanted from him was protection, and all he'd done was put her and her child in more danger.

Blood stained the crumpled dash of the SUV. The chief flinched as he studied the wreckage. "I want this processed right away," he told the tech from the crime lab.

The young woman's eyes widened with surprise. She had to be wondering why a traffic accident would take precedence over all of their other cases. But this hadn't been an accident.

Forrest had been right to take the threat to Rae Lemmon's child seriously. Detective Colton had paid for protecting them with his own blood. Jonah and Donovan had assured him that their brother was fine. But now that he'd seen the crash for himself…

It could have been so much worse. The baby could have been hurt, as well. Despite his sleepless night of surveillance, Forrest had done a damn fine job of minimizing the risk to other drivers on the road and to that child. Maybe Austin PD shouldn't have been so damn quick to retire him with disability. The detective was more physically capable than his previous department and maybe he himself knew.

"We're also looking for a white van," he told the tech. "If one turns up—"

"Over there, Chief," the tech interrupted as she pointed to another corner of the police impound lot.

Smoke rose yet from the burned-out skeleton of a vehicle, and a groan slipped through his lips.

"I'm not sure it was white," the tech said. "It was already fully engaged when the fire department was called to an alley not far from the hospital."

Had the driver followed the ambulance to the ER? Had he wanted to make certain that Forrest or the baby hadn't survived the crash?

"We need that processed ASAP, as well," he said.

"We'll have to wait until it cools off, Chief," the tech pointed out.

He nodded. "Just until…" He needed a damn lead to whoever had threatened his new detective. He couldn't lose Forrest yet, but he suspected that he would eventually—to another, longer-term job.

His cell phone vibrated in his pocket. He pulled it out and expelled a sigh when he saw the screen. It was Forrest. Was he already leaving?

After Archer hadn't taken his concerns seriously, he might be compelled to quit. He walked back to his SUV before clicking the accept button. "Colton, how are you?" he asked.

"So you know," Forrest said.

"I'm at the impound lot now," he admitted. "You're lucky you walked away from that crash." Then he flinched at his insensitivity. He'd been told that it was lucky that Forrest could walk at all—after the shooting that had nearly ended his career and his life.

"That's not the only thing I should walk away from," Forrest said.

And Archer swallowed a curse before asking, "You're quitting?"

"Yes," Forrest replied.

"But I thought you wanted to find the killer, too." Not as much as Archer did, though. Nobody wanted to find the killer as much as he did. All those years he'd spent wondering what had happened to his sister...

Was her killer the same one who'd buried the body near the parking lot of the drug company, though? Or were there two of them?

And if so, he needed Forrest Colton now more than ever. "You can't give up yet."

"I'm not giving up on finding the killer," Forrest assured him. "I'm giving up protection duty."

Archer glanced over at the wreckage and sighed. "Of course. I don't blame you." Not after that crash. Even though his offer came too late, he said, "I'll send over an officer to replace you."

"Who?" Forrest asked.

"I don't know yet," Archer said. "I'll have to see who's coming on duty, so they can stay through the night."

"Only send someone who's done this kind of thing before," Forrest suggested.

Or was it an order?

Forrest unwittingly answered the chief's unspoken question when he added, "Whoever you send will need to meet my approval."

He clicked off before Archer could comment further, leaving the chief wondering if anyone he sent would actually meet Forrest's approval. Just how attached had the young detective gotten to Rae Lemmon and her baby?

Rae sucked in a breath at the sudden jab of pain in her chest. It was as if Forrest had plunged a knife into her heart. He was leaving just like every other man she'd ever known.

How could he? But then how could she think that he would stay after he'd been hurt? After his sleepless night? After what he'd said about putting her and Connor in more danger with his presence?

He must have felt her presence, because he turned away from the back door and the window he'd been staring through while he'd spoken to the chief.

"You're really leaving," she murmured.

He nodded. "Once my replacement arrives."

Her skin heated with a sudden surge of anger. She wasn't as angry with him, though, as she was with herself. Last night never should have happened; she never should have trusted him enough to make love with him.

"So much for your promise," she bitterly remarked.

"I will make sure you and Connor stay safe," he assured her. "And the most effective way for me to do that is to stay away from the two of you."

A twinge of pain joined her anger. "So leave then," she told him. "We don't need you." But her words echoed hollowly back to her. How had she, in such a short amount of time, become reliant on him?

She had always been so independent. That had

begun out of necessity, but it was her choice now. To be alone.

"Leave," she ordered him.

His vehicle was here, since they'd taken hers that morning because the baby carrier had already been buckled into the back seat. And hers was the one that had been wrecked.

"I'm not leaving until my replacement gets here," he said. "I'm keeping my promise."

She snorted. "You're keeping your distance. What? You get scared today?"

"Yes," he said.

She wasn't sure if he was talking about the crash or something else.

Her?

"I was scared that something had happened to your son," he said. "That I had broken that promise you didn't even want me to make to you. And that scared me. It scared me that I care about him, about you."

She gasped now, as shock surged through her, replacing the anger. "Forrest…" She stepped closer to him, but like when she had reached for him earlier, he moved away from her.

It was as if he couldn't bear her touch anymore.

That hadn't been the case last night.

Last night he'd uttered a ragged groan every time she'd touched him, kissed him…

"It's because I care that I have to stay away from you," he said.

Realization dawned. He wasn't talking about just protecting her; he was talking about making love to her.

He didn't want to do it again.

He considered last night a mistake.

So should she—because it had made her want something she should have already known wasn't possible.

Someone she could count on.

Chapter 15

The young officer seemed capable enough. Since he'd worked as a security guard while putting himself through college and the police academy, he had experience with protection duty. He also looked like a body builder, so he was probably a hell of a lot more capable than Forrest was. But the thought of leaving churned his guts so much that he felt physically sick. He wasn't ready to leave yet, so he'd sent the young officer outside to patrol the yard.

That was probably the best place for him to be with the sun setting. It had taken the chief a while even to send someone out and a while longer for Forrest to interview the man. During that time he had seen very little of Rae.

Connor had awakened, and she'd busied herself by

taking care of him and ignoring Forrest's presence. Or at least that was how he felt: ignored. Like she wanted to pretend he'd already left, like her father had left.

Was that why she'd gotten so upset about his turning over her protection duty to someone else? Because she figured he'd broken his promise like her dad had broken his promise to stand beside her mother through sickness and health?

He didn't want to be compared to a person like that, to someone who reminded him so much of his own ex-fiancée. Shannon certainly hadn't wanted to stick around during his sickness.

But Rae and Connor weren't sick. They were in danger. Because of him.

The best thing he could do to protect them was to stay away from them. Surely, she had to see that was why he'd chosen to turn over the duty of guarding them to someone else. Someone like the capable, young officer outside.

He glanced out the window, but it had gotten so dark that he couldn't see Officer Baker anymore. He could have called him, made certain he was still out there and then he could have left. But thinking about her father had made him curious about the man.

How long ago had Mr. Lemmon taken off?

Around the time that body had been buried in his backyard? Since it had been mummified, it could have been there for decades, like the chief's sister's body had been. It could have been there before Rae's parents had even moved into this house. But what if it hadn't been?

What if that body had had more to do with Rae's

dad taking off than his wife's illness? Maybe he'd been running away from the scene of his crime.

Crimes?

Had he known Emmeline Thompson, too?

Wanting to ask all those questions, Forrest glanced toward the closed door to Rae's bedroom. That must have been shut as a message to him, because she hadn't closed it the night before. But then he'd been in that bedroom with her for much of last night. He'd been in that bed with her.

He longed to join her now in her bed, but he doubted she would welcome his presence. Or even the questions now swirling through his head. So instead of looking for answers from her, he began to look for them around the house.

This was where Rae had grown up, where she'd lived with her mother, and her father had lived there, too—before he'd taken off. Frames held photos of her mother and of Rae at different ages. But where were the photos of her father?

Forrest rose from the kitchen chair, grimacing over the pain shooting up and down his stiffened leg. He stood for a long moment before he trusted it to hold him as he walked. Then he headed out of the kitchen and into the living room. On the wall opposite to Rae's closed bedroom door was a row of bookshelves. He hobbled toward those because he'd spied earlier, among the spines of books, a couple of photo albums.

Leg still aching in protest of his weight, he dropped onto the sofa next to the bookshelves and flipped open the first album. Dust fell off the top of the plastic folders and settled onto his dark pants.

Rae must not have looked at these photos in a long time. Then he realized why when he saw the man in the pictures. He had to be Rae's father—not that they looked much alike, but in some of the photographs, he was holding a baby that looked like Connor in a pink blanket, and in a few others, he was holding the hand of a little girl with big dark eyes and brown hair who gazed adoringly up at him.

There were also photos of him with a woman who looked like a taller, willowy version of Rae. But he looked distracted in some of those photos, as his attention was either on the television or something in his hand.

Forrest leaned over the album, peering at the slips of paper. In other photos, those pieces of paper were either sticking out of his pocket or wadded up in his hands.

Betting slips?

But what did that mean?

Had Beau Lemmon been a bookie or a gambler?

And how did that relate to the mummified body in his backyard? Had that person owed him a debt? Or had he owed one to her?

Had Beau Lemmon killed that person and buried her in his own backyard, where his adorable little girl had played?

Forrest had already pegged the guy for a loser, taking off when his wife got sick, but now he wondered if he was more than that.

A killer.

* * *

Was he gone? She'd heard the other officer arrive, had heard them speak and then a door opened and closed. Had Forrest turned over Connor's and her security to another bodyguard?

After the day he'd had, she couldn't entirely blame him. The anger she'd felt earlier with him had faded now to disappointment and disillusionment.

She'd made a mistake being intimate with him last night. Just as she'd had in the past with other men. Having sex didn't lead to true intimacy, not the kind her friends had found with their Colton men.

She'd thought he might be worth risking her heart on.

A twinge of pain struck it now. How had she already let herself start falling for him?

She knew better. She knew that—at least for the women in her family—love didn't last, if it had ever really been love at all. And in her case—with Forrest—she hardly knew him. So of course it wasn't love.

It was appreciation for how sweet and protective he'd been with Connor. That was all it was.

And desire.

Her body ached with that now, so much that she couldn't sleep. Not without him.

Resigned to another restless night, she threw back the thin sheet and rolled out of bed. She should have introduced herself to the officer. Actually, she should have been the one who'd interviewed him. After all, he was assigned to protect her and Connor. Not Forrest.

He was going to stay away from them.

For their sakes?

Or his?

She suspected it was as much for his as it was for theirs. Was he afraid of getting hurt physically again or emotionally?

That fear of his getting hurt flickered through her. The note writer wanted him gone to the extent that he'd tried to take Forrest's life.

Maybe his staying away was for the best—for him. Maybe he should leave Whisperwood entirely. Maybe he already had.

She grabbed her robe from the back of the door and shoved her arms into the sleeves. After securing the tie around her waist, she pulled open the door and stepped into the living room.

A wave of relief rushed over her. He hadn't left. He sat on her couch, a lock of light brown hair falling across his forehead as his head bent over something on his lap. When she identified what it was, her relief fled, leaving only panic and pain.

"What are you doing?" she asked.

He didn't jump or tense. He must have noticed when she'd opened the door, but he hadn't looked over at her. He didn't even look up at her now. Instead he was totally focused on those old photographs.

"Why are you looking at those?" she asked with a shudder of her own. She didn't like looking at them, at the past. The only photographs she wanted to see were the ones hanging on her walls or sitting in frames on the shelves. Maybe she should have tossed out the old photo albums, but she'd figured that one day her children might want to see pictures of her past, to learn more about it.

Why did Forrest?

"Do you know where he is?" he asked, and he pointed toward a picture of her father.

She sucked in a breath and shook her head. But because he still wasn't looking at her, she replied shortly and succinctly, "No."

"No idea?"

"I don't think about it," she said. "I don't think about him."

He looked up at her then, his deep hazel eyes filled with skepticism of her claim.

With good reason, she had lied. She thought about him, about how he'd taken off on her and her mom, every time she considered risking her heart on someone. Like Forrest.

She remembered how Beau Lemmon had hurt her mother and her, and she realized that falling in love wasn't worth the inevitable pain that followed the fall.

"Let's just say I don't know, and I don't care," she said.

He tilted his head, and his eyes narrowed. "Have you heard from him?"

She shook her head.

"Nothing?" he asked. "Not even when your mother died? Didn't he try to inherit the house or—"

"Mom was sick for a long time. She divorced him during that time and made sure I was her sole beneficiary," she explained. Her mother hadn't been bitter about Beau, but she'd been realistic.

"Why?" he asked. "Did she think he would just gamble it all away if he inherited?" And he pointed to something in the picture, a slip of paper.

"Lottery ticket?" she asked.

He shook his head. "More like a betting slip—serious gambling."

She snorted. "Serious? I don't think that's something my father ever was."

Not even when he'd made those promises that he would come back to them a better man. If he'd been serious, he would have come back. If he'd been able…

"I think he might have been serious about gambling," Forrest said. "Maybe he went to Vegas or Reno when he left Whisperwood."

She shrugged. "I don't know. He didn't leave a forwarding address."

"And he's never sent a letter or postcard?" Forrest persisted.

She snorted. "My father isn't like yours. He wasn't a good man or a…" She trailed off as she realized the reason for his questions. "You think he buried that body in the backyard?"

"I do consider him a suspect," Forrest admitted.

She appreciated his honesty even as she felt a flash of shame. "When I said my father isn't a good man, I wasn't implying that he's a bad man. That he's evil. He's just flawed."

Most people were.

As if thinking of his flaw, Forrest rubbed his palm over his wounded leg.

She'd run her lips over it, over the scars from the

bullets and from the surgeries that had pieced his leg back together. But that wound wasn't a flaw. There was nothing flawed about Forrest Colton.

He was so damn good-looking with that chiseled jaw and cheekbones and those deep-set hazel eyes. He stared up at her again, and his eyes darkened even more as the pupils dilated and swallowed up all of the gold and green.

As if he'd read her mind, he murmured, "You're not flawed." Then, despite the obvious discomfort of his leg, he surged to his feet. "You're absolutely flawless."

When he looked at her the way he was looking, the way he'd looked at her last night, she believed that he found her as irresistible as she found him. And he was irresistible. So irresistible that she heaved a heavy sigh before she stepped closer to him and wrapped her arms around him. Then she rose on tiptoe and brushed her mouth across his.

He sucked in a breath. "I thought you were mad at me for leaving."

Her lips tugged up into a smile as she pointed out the obvious, "You're still here."

He heaved a heavy sigh now that feathered through her tangled hair. "I know."

"Why?"

"Because I can't bring myself to leave."

He would. Eventually. She knew that. Everybody had left Rae—whether they'd intended to, like her father and some ex-boyfriends, or they hadn't intended to, like her mother, who'd fought so hard to beat the cancer. But it had kept coming back for her.

She closed her eyes as a wave of pain washed over her. Forrest must have seen it, because he closed his arms around her and softly asked, "Are you okay?"

She gestured at the couch. "That—those pictures—just bring up painful memories."

He moved one hand from her back to her face and ran his fingers along her jaw. "Then let's make better memories—like last night. That's all I've been able to think about. You. Being with you. Being *inside* you."

She shivered even as her flesh heated and her pulse pounded. "Yes," she murmured.

"I haven't asked a question," he said, and he was smiling now.

"You will," she said. He'd made certain last night, several times, that she really wanted him. To save them time, she told him, "I want you. I want you with me, inside me."

He groaned and bent forward slightly, as if she'd kicked him. But then he straightened up and lifted her into his arms as he did.

"Forrest," she protested. "Your leg—"

"I don't care," he said. "I don't care about anything but getting you to that damn bed."

She giggled despite her concern. She giggled at his eagerness. He clearly wanted her as badly as she did him. Despite his injury and his limp, he carried her easily and quickly to the bedroom and to the bed.

Maybe he dropped her a little abruptly onto the mattress, so abruptly that she bounced once, but she only giggled again. He hadn't dropped her because he was hurting—at least not over his leg or his head. He'd dropped her because he was tearing off his clothes to join her. To join them.

As he laid his holstered gun on the table beside her bed, he murmured, "There's a police officer outside. You and Connor are safe."

She couldn't help but wonder if he was trying to convince her or himself. She didn't care, though. She cared only about being with him, as naked as he was now. So she shrugged off her robe and pulled her T-shirt over her head.

He sucked in a breath as his pupils dilated and his nostrils flared. "You are so damn beautiful."

Her hair was a mess, and her makeup all washed off, but he didn't seem to care—not with the way he stared at her, as if awed.

He made her feel beautiful. She smiled as pride swelled within her. But then she looked at him, standing so gloriously naked beside the bed, and she was suddenly humbled. He was all sculpted muscles—but for the scarred leg. But that only made him more attractive, since it was a badge of his courage and his determination. He was a hero.

Her hero.

She reached out for him, tugging him down onto the bed with her. She wrapped her arms around his neck and pulled his head down to hers. She kissed him with all of the desire raging inside her.

He kissed her back just as hungrily, his mouth moving sensually across her. His lips nipped at and nibbled hers. Pulling her bottom lip between his, he nipped at it lightly with his teeth before sliding his tongue across it and then into her mouth.

He made love to her mouth like she wanted him to make love to her body.

She arched up, rubbing her hips and breasts against him. His erection throbbed against her belly, pulsating with his passion.

"Forrest," she murmured against his mouth.

Then he moved his mouth, sliding his lips down her throat to the point where her pulse pounded madly with desire. Her heart racing, she nearly sobbed at the tension building inside her.

His soft hair tickled her skin as he moved his head lower, to her breasts. He kissed the full mounds before closing his lips over a taut nipple.

She cried out with pleasure as he tugged on it. Then he slid his tongue across it, and that pleasure flowed from the tip of her breast to her core, which pulsated with need. "Forrest…"

But he was moving again, his mouth sliding across her belly and over her mound. Then he touched her core, his tongue stroking over the most sensitive part of her.

She cried out softly as she came. But it wasn't enough.

She wanted more.

She wanted him.

All of him.

Filling her, like he had last night. Filling the emptiness she hadn't even realized she'd had, the hollow ache that she hadn't been aware of until he'd filled her, until he'd completed her.

He pulled back and fumbled around beside the bed. She spied the packet in his hand and took it from him. After tearing it open, she rolled the condom onto his throbbing erection.

He groaned as cords stood out in his neck and along his temple. "Rae, you're killing me."

She didn't want to do that, but someone did. Someone had tried...

She could have lost him. The thought filled her with horror and dread. And she reached out for him, clasping him closely, pressing kisses to his mouth and then his neck and his shoulder and his chest.

A growl emanated from his throat, and he lifted her as he crouched on the bed. Then he guided himself inside her.

As he filled her, she came again, her inner muscles clutching at him. He groaned and thrust again and again until he joined her in pleasure.

So much damn pleasure...

She'd never felt anything so intense, never known such pleasure existed. But he wasn't done—even though they'd both climaxed.

He kept touching her, kissing her, making her fall deeper and deeper in love with him. And now he was killing her—with pleasure.

Forrest Colton wasn't dead.

He should have been furious that his order hadn't been carried out. But just that attempt on Colton's life and the threats against the woman seemed to have distracted him from his cases.

So those threats and those attempts would have to keep happening to keep Detective Colton distracted. And if one of those attempts happened to succeed…

A grin curved his lips. He wouldn't give a damn about another life lost, since he hadn't given a damn about the first.

The only life he wanted to protect was his own.

Chapter 16

A week had passed of Forrest keeping his distance from Rae and Connor. It was for the best—for them and for him. And probably for Whisperwood, as well. He could focus on his cases again.

He could focus on finding a killer who was probably the same person who'd run him and Connor off the road. The person who'd left those threats for Rae.

Her father?

Why would he have been gone for all of these years only to return and threaten her? It made no sense. But still...

He'd put out an APB for Beau Lemmon to be picked up for questioning. Forrest had a hell of a lot of questions for him. Like how he'd walked out on his sick wife and daughter, and how much he knew about that body buried in his backyard.

Rae's backyard now. The house was hers, along with whatever other estate her mother had left her. Would her father resent her over that enough to threaten her?

Realizing he was grasping at straws, Forrest sighed and focused on the other files on his desk. Patrice Eccleston's file. He wished it was thicker than it was, but the leads and clues were slim.

He still hadn't gotten back the lab results on those buttons, coins or whatever the hell it was he'd found at both crime scenes. The presence at both of them should have proved that the same killer had murdered the victims. But why had one body been mummified and the other not?

His head began to pound, and it had nothing to do with the yellowing bruise on his forehead. The bump had gone down, like the one on his knee. Frustration, not physical wounds, caused his aches. And not just frustration with the murder cases.

He was frustrated over not seeing Rae, over not being with Rae. He missed Connor, too, missed the innocence of the infant and the warmth and even the scent of him.

Powder and soap and…sometimes things that weren't all that sweet. His lips curved into a slight grin as he remembered the baby's spitting up all over his shirt.

And what that had led to.

He and Rae making love.

God, he missed her. So damn much.

"What the hell are you doing?" a voice demanded to know. "Daydreaming? You should be out tracking down my sister's killer, not snoozing behind your desk."

Ian Eccleston loomed over the partition wall of Forrest's cubicle in the Whisperwood Police Department. He didn't have a private office. Since he was only temporary, he was probably lucky he'd even been given a desk.

He snapped the folder shut and flipped it over so Ian wouldn't see the label that had the victim's name beneath the case number. He didn't want Patrice's brother to see how little information they had.

He also had a strange feeling about Ian Eccleston. Maybe his anger was just one of the stages of grief. Or maybe it was something else.

"Do you have anything to share with me?" Forrest asked him. "Something you've remembered about your sister?"

The guy's face flushed as his temper grew hotter yet. "That's your job. I'm not doing your job for you."

"You want your sister's killer caught, don't you?" Forrest asked.

The guy jerked his head in a quick nod. "Yeah, but I ain't the detective. You are—though I checked you out, Colton, and all you do is cold cases."

"That was my last assignment with the Austin Police Department," he reminded the guy. "Not my only one."

"But you're probably focusing on those cold cases—those old bodies—not my sister's fresh one." He flinched as he said it, so maybe the guy really cared that his sister was dead. Or maybe this was all an act to throw suspicion off him.

Forrest flinched now at his own cynicism. When had he begun to suspect everyone? Why couldn't he look at people the way Rae did? Just because someone wasn't necessarily good didn't mean they were bad. They were just flawed. Maybe Ian Eccleston was just flawed, or maybe he was justifiably furious that his sister's killer was still running around free.

And she was dead.

Forrest tapped his fingers against that turned-over folder with the photos inside of her crime scene, of her corpse. No. Her brother didn't need to see the contents of her file, whether he was grieving or the killer.

He wasn't old enough to have committed the other murders, though. But he could have heard enough about them recently to try to copycat one.

Was that what Patrice's murder was? A copycat or the killer's comeback murder?

Had Beau Lemmon come back to Whisperwood?

"What are you doing to find Patrice's killer?" her brother asked.

"I'm not at liberty to discuss ongoing investigations," Forrest said.

Ian snorted. "That's the answer you and the chief keep giving in interviews," he said. "I'm not some nosy reporter. I have a right to know what you're doing to find my sister's killer."

Bracing his hand against the folder on his desk, Forrest used it to push himself up from his chair. Maybe he would need to walk Ian to the door. But before he could move away from his desk, a young female officer rushed up to them.

"Everything all right?" she asked as she glanced toward his unannounced visitor.

How had Ian gotten back to his cubicle?

Forrest nodded. "Mr. Eccleston was leaving."

"I'm not going anywhere until you give me some answers," Ian stubbornly insisted.

Forrest regretfully admitted, "I don't have any answers to give you."

Ian snorted. "And you're supposed to be some hotshot Austin detective."

"I do have that information you requested on Beau Lemmon," the officer said, as if in Forrest's defense. "I emailed it to you."

"Do you know where he is?" he asked.

She shook her head.

"Beau Lemmon?" Ian asked, his forehead furrowed with confusion.

"Do you know him?" Forrest asked. "Did your sister know him?"

"No." Ian cursed. "This has nothing to do with her, does it?"

"We have several open cases," the officer answered for Forrest.

She might have thought she was helping him, but she only made Ian more furious. His face flushed an even brighter shade of red.

"And every one of those cases is more important to you than my sister is," Ian angrily exclaimed. He cursed both of them then before rushing out of the department.

"I'm sorry," the officer said.

He shook his head. "Not your fault." It was his for not finding Patrice's killer. "You weren't able to find Beau Lemmon yet?"

She sighed. "No, I'm sorry. But I did find some arrests on his record, which will give you an idea of where he's been and what he's been doing."

Forrest tapped his keyboard and pulled up his email. He found hers and opened the attachments, the arrest reports from Las Vegas PD and Reno PD and Atlantic City.

He sure as hell had pegged Beau Lemmon right. The guy was a gambler. But his arrests weren't for gambling—at least not directly. The money he'd stolen as a pickpocket and through breaking and entering had probably been to finance his gambling or to pay off debts.

If he was desperate enough to steal, what else might he be desperate enough to do? Kill?

The officer pulled out his gun and pointed it at the door as someone stepped onto the porch.

"You can put that away," Rae said. "It's just one of my bosses from the law office."

Kenneth Dawson tapped his fingers lightly against the glass in the door before turning the knob. Rae gasped at his audacity. Maybe she shouldn't have had the officer re-holster his weapon. Catching the knob in her hand, she held it tightly, got behind the door and pulled it open just a few inches. But Kenneth pushed against it, trying to open it wider as he peered inside her house.

"What are you doing here?" she asked. She'd been working from home, but all her assignments had been emailed to her, not personally delivered.

"We're missing you at the office," he said. "Wanted to make sure everything was okay."

Maybe that was why he seemed so nosy. Or maybe that was just his personality—since he was the only one at the firm who fit the unflattering description of lawyers being ambulance chasers. Had he chased one here?

Had someone found another body nearby? She couldn't see around him, though, since he blocked the entire doorway, trying to force his way inside.

Knowing the officer was close, she stepped back and let him in the door. He tensed as he noticed the young officer standing behind her. She was glad that it was Officer Baker's shift; the guy was bigger than some body builders.

"Looks like I was right to check up on you," Kenneth said. "Is everything okay?"

Officer Baker didn't say anything. Maybe he wasn't allowed to comment.

Rae had already told the law-firm partners about the threats and that she didn't want to put anyone else at work in danger with her presence. Hadn't they shared that information with Kenneth?

And if not, why not?

Didn't they trust him?

Should she?

He had never actually done anything that had made her uncomfortable, though, until the other day. Something about the way he'd looked at her, and the questions he'd asked her about Forrest—it had all felt inappropriate to her.

Like his showing up here.

"Detective Colton is concerned about my safety," she said.

"Detective Colton," he repeated the name, his voice sharp with something like resentment.

But why would he resent Forrest? He was older than Forrest—probably at least a decade older—so they hadn't grown up together. Their paths could have crossed in law enforcement, though.

"Where is Detective Colton now?" Kenneth asked, and he glanced around her house, as if looking for him.

She flinched. Forrest had said he was going to stay away for her and Connor's safety. But she suspected he was just avoiding her. While he desired her, he obviously didn't want the responsibility of a ready-made family.

When she'd chosen to become a single mother, she'd known that some men might be turned off by the prospect of raising a child that wasn't theirs. But she'd figured she wouldn't be interested in those men anyway. That wasn't the case with Forrest. She was more than just interested in him; she was infatuated.

"You and the detective aren't on a first-name basis?" Kenneth asked, a smirk twisting his thin lips.

Heat rushed to her face, but she was not about to

discuss her relationship with Forrest with a colleague. Not that she had a relationship with him. She hadn't even heard from him over the past week.

But he always called whatever officer was guarding her at the moment. Predictably this officer's phone rang. Baker pulled it out and, as he glanced at the screen, remarked, "This is Detective Colton now. I should take this."

He hesitated, though, before clicking the accept button. "Will you be okay if I step outside?" he asked.

She wanted to tell him no, but she didn't want to offend Kenneth. His father-in-law was one of the partners. Because of that, surely she could trust him not to try anything with her. After all he was married to his boss's daughter.

She nodded. "Sure, I'll be fine."

"Of course she will," Kenneth told the officer, using his hand to wave him off.

The young man's brow furrowed, but the phone continued to ring, so he opened the door and stepped onto the porch. As the door closed behind him, panic settled on Rae's chest. Maybe it was just that she hadn't been without security the past week, or maybe it was that something about Kenneth scared her now.

Before she could figure out the reason for her uneasiness, a cry emanated from the nursery. She nearly breathed a sigh of relief as she hurried toward her son. As she leaned over the crib railing to pick him up, she heard a strange noise and turned around to find that Kenneth had followed her.

And he was staring at her ass as she leaned over her

child. Too bad she was wearing shorts instead of jeans. She hurriedly picked up Connor and turned so that her son was a shield between her and her colleague.

But Kenneth stepped forward and reached for one of Connor's kicking feet. "Look at you, you're so cute," he cooed.

Connor stiffened and cried louder with either fear or dislike. He was apparently not a fan of Kenneth's either. Not that she hadn't been…until that day she'd found the threat on her desk and Forrest and Connor had been run off the road. But maybe that had just made her paranoid.

"He's not a happy baby, huh?" Kenneth remarked.

"Usually he is," she said. With the exception of those colicky nights he'd kept her awake. He'd never cried when Forrest had touched him; in fact he'd stopped crying for Forrest.

But Forrest wasn't here. And he probably wasn't coming back—even after he caught the killer. Because once the killer was caught, he would be able to leave. Return to his job in Austin or find a permanent job somewhere else.

She pushed that thought from her mind as she focused on her child. She changed him into a dry diaper and onesie, but he didn't stop crying.

"Is he hungry?" Kenneth asked. "Do you need to breastfeed?" His gaze dropped to her chest, as if he expected her to start right now, right in front of him.

"I don't breastfeed anymore," she said. Just because of the stress of her busy schedule, she hadn't been able to produce much milk. And now with the stress of those threats and the danger she and Connor were in, she hadn't been able to produce any at all.

"Poor little guy," Kenneth said with a smirk. "No wonder he's unhappy."

She couldn't suppress the shudder of revulsion over his comment. "I need to take care of him," she said, "so you should probably leave."

"But I came all this way to check on you," he said.

"And I'm fine," she said. Thanks to Forrest's making sure she had protection.

But now Forrest's phone call had drawn that protection away from her. She had a feeling she might need him back…because Kenneth kept coming closer.

She didn't want to lose her job, but she wasn't going to tolerate any harassment either. "I can't remember—do you and your wife have children?" she asked.

He shuddered now. "God, no."

She sucked in a breath.

"I just mean—we're too young," he said.

He was older than she was.

"And too busy," he added.

His wife didn't work. Neither of them was as busy as Rae was. But she wouldn't judge him for not wanting children any more than she wanted people judging her for wanting them so much that she'd chosen to raise her son alone.

"I know you're busy," she said. "So I appreciate you stopping by to check on me. But I wouldn't want to keep you."

His blue eyes narrowed now, as it must have finally occurred to him that she was trying to get rid of him.

"What's the matter, Rae? Don't you want me in your house?"

She suspected that wasn't where he really wanted to be. He wanted to be where Forrest had been—in her bed. But Forrest had left her bed and never returned.

She didn't want any other man in it, though. Especially after that.

She was never going to trust another man to get that close to her. But Kenneth was leaning closer, over Connor.

With a silent plea for forgiveness, she thrust her son into his arms. "You want to hold him?"

The baby squirmed and screamed in his awkward embrace. And he hurriedly handed back her son. "No, no, I don't want to hold him."

Forrest hadn't reacted like that when she'd thrust Connor into his arms that first morning he'd showed up in her backyard. He'd held him and soothed him better than she'd been able to.

He was so good with Connor. And with her.

But it didn't seem like he was ever coming back. She didn't want Kenneth to come back either.

"You're lucky he didn't throw up on you," she said with a slight smile. "He has a tendency to do that."

Kenneth recoiled even more. "Well, I better be going then." He walked out of the nursery, but instead of heading to the front door, he walked to the back door and peered into the yard.

"Your car is out front," she reminded him as she followed him into the kitchen.

"Crime scene's out there," he murmured, as he

stared at the hole in the ground. Yellow tape dangled from posts that had been pounded into the ground around it. "So that's where the body was found."

Again, it wasn't a question. He knew.

From what he'd heard on the police scanner? Or for another reason?

Even though the air-conditioning wasn't doing much to cool the house, she shivered. She hated this, hated suspecting everyone around her.

But there was just something so damn creepy about Kenneth now. But was he creepy enough to be a killer?

Chapter 17

Maybe it was Ian's visit earlier that day that had un-
settled Forrest. Or had it been his phone call to the officer on protection duty that had done it?

What the hell had Kenneth Dawson been doing at
Rae's house? He could have been bringing her work.
But wasn't most office work done electronically now?
Forrest suspected work wasn't why Kenneth had stopped
by; he'd wanted to see Rae.

Forrest did, too. Maybe that was the reason for his
current state of restlessness. A week was just too damn
long for him to go without seeing Rae and Connor,
without personally making sure that they were all right.
Without touching her, kissing her…being with her…

Not that he expected her to welcome him back
into her arms or her bed. She probably felt that he'd

abandoned her, the way her father had abandoned her mother when she'd needed him most. But Rae didn't really need Forrest.

Nobody did.

Other—more able-bodied—officers would do a better job protecting her and Connor. Forrest couldn't chase down a suspect—couldn't run off a threat—the way the more physically capable officers could.

And those other officers weren't in danger like Forrest was either. They wouldn't endanger her and Connor with their very presence like he did.

But nothing else had happened to him after he and Connor had been run off the road. Nobody had made another attempt on his life. So maybe the person just wanted him out of Rae's and Connor's lives.

But why?

So he could insinuate himself there? Like Kenneth Dawson might have tried this afternoon? Had that been the purpose of his visit? Or had he been scoping out the situation to return later?

A chill chased down Forrest's spine with the horrific thought. Maybe no more attempts had been made in the past week because the killer had been taking his time to plot his next attack so that he would succeed.

But what was his goal? To get rid of Forrest or of Rae and Connor?

Nobody knew this place better than he did. Hell, he was the only one who knew the body had been buried here. Well, not the only one.

The discovery of that body should have served as

a big enough distraction, should have kept the damn police department busy trying to figure out who the victim was and what had happened to her. But it hadn't been enough.

At least not to the person who now held his debt. He—whoever the hell he was—wanted more from him. Wanted blood.

Murder.

He'd almost pulled it off when he'd forced the detective to drive into that parked car. But somehow Detective Colton had survived. So had the baby.

Not that he'd wanted to hurt the baby. He hadn't. But he didn't want to get hurt either.

And that was going to happen if he didn't do more to get rid of Colton. He had to send the stubborn detective a real message. A message that no matter what Forrest Colton did—or how many people he had protecting the house—Rae and the baby weren't safe.

Nobody was.

Keeping to the shadows, he moved closer to the back of the house. The plastic tape strewn around that hole fluttered in the slight breeze. He didn't need the tape to know where that hole was; he'd dug up most of it himself. And a few other damn holes before he'd remembered where it was.

Rae hadn't seen him then. She hadn't seen him once since he had returned to Whisperwood. Maybe that needed to change.

Maybe he needed to talk to her—to make her understand...

But to get close to her, he had to get rid of her protection. The moonlight illuminated most of the yard, enough that he could see a rock lying among the mound of dirt. He picked it up in his gloved hand and tossed it, not at the house, but at the barbecue grill sitting on the back patio.

Metal clanged. And a light came on inside the kitchen, and then another beside the back door that illuminated the patio. His heart pounding, he ducked into the shadows again. He had to do this, had to be ready. So he reached into his back pocket, where he'd tucked another weapon—a long pipe—and he pulled that out. And he waited.

It didn't take the officer long to open the door and step onto the patio. He came out with his gun drawn, though. A pipe would be no match for a bullet.

So he needed the element of surprise. Too bad he hadn't picked up two damn rocks.

But as fate would have it, something else moved in the darkness. Undoubtedly an animal.

It rustled the brush just beyond the hole in the yard and drew the officer farther from the house. With his gun pointing toward the brush, he walked right past the shadows where his assailant hid.

Once he passed, his assailant struck out, swinging the pipe at the back of his head. It connected hard, knocking him to the ground.

He made no sound.

No movement.

Was he unconscious or dead?

A twinge of regret struck his heart, which most people probably suspected he didn't even possess. But he had one. As always, though, most of his love was for himself. He was a hell of lot more concerned about his own life than anyone else's.

So he left the officer lying on the ground, and he headed toward the house. After he closed his hand around the knob of the back door, he tried to turn it, but it refused to budge. The damn cop had locked it behind himself.

Maybe he'd suspected the noise had been a ruse to draw him out of the house. Maybe he'd already called for backup in case he didn't return.

But what if he had locked it, he must have had a key on him—some way to get back inside the house. The key was no longer under the pot on the front porch.

If only that had been Colton's skull he'd struck with the pipe…

If the officer had called for backup, it probably would have been Colton. So maybe there would be a chance to strike him yet.

To get rid of him for good.

If the officer hadn't called him, Rae would when she heard him coming. So he swung his pipe again, this time at the window in the locked door. The sound of glass breaking shattered the quiet of the night.

The officer had already warned Rae that he was heading outside to investigate a noise he'd heard. He'd locked the door behind himself and had advised her to open it only for him. He'd only been gone moments when someone had tried to turn the knob. He'd known it was locked; he'd locked it himself.

So he wouldn't have done that, not without alerting her first. He wasn't the one trying to open that door. Fear coursing through her, she'd headed toward the nursery, where Connor was sleeping. Or had been sleeping.

The tinkling explosion of shattered glass awakened him with a scream on his lips. Rae didn't go right to his crib, though. Instead she closed and locked his door behind her.

But was the lock enough?

It was one of those that could be picked with a paperclip. So she pushed her shoulder against his dresser, sliding it across the floor—the legs of it scraping the wood—until it blocked the door. But she'd been able to move it, and she wasn't very big. Someone else would surely be able to move it aside to get to them.

Heart pounding with panic, she rushed around the room, grabbing things to pile on or push against the dresser. She had to make it impossible to move. She had to keep out the threat against her son and her.

But what about the young officer?

What had happened to him?

Was he okay?

She needed to call for help for him and for them. But her house was so far from town that it would be too late for help to arrive—if she didn't manage to keep the intruder out of the nursery.

Away from Connor.

Guilt tore at her—over the officer, over Connor's crying.

And tears stung her eyes, blurring her vision. She

blinked them back. She had to be able to see as she pulled her phone from the pocket of her robe.

She should have called for help the minute the officer had stepped outside. Or she should have insisted that he wait for backup before going out there. But he'd shrugged off her concern, assuring her that it was probably just an animal that had made the noise.

It had been.

The human kind of animal—the kind who kills young women and threatens babies and…

She flinched at the thought of what could have happened to the cop. Her fingers trembling, she could barely work her phone, but she managed to find the emergency call button.

A dispatcher would find a close officer—would send the person who could get to the house the fastest. That person wasn't Forrest.

She had no idea where he was or what he was doing. But even if he'd been close, she wouldn't want him here. She didn't want whatever had happened to that officer to happen to Forrest. He'd already been hurt once because of her; she didn't want him hurt again.

"9-1-1. What's your emergency?" asked a voice emanating from her phone.

She could barely hear it over Connor's crying and now over the sound of someone banging against her door.

"Someone's broken in to my house," Rae said. "And I think they hurt an officer—"

"There was already an officer at the scene?"

"Yes," Rae said. Then, knowing that it wasn't always

possible for GPS locating to work in her area, she gave her name and address. "Please hurry!"

But no matter how close other police officers were, they wouldn't get to her and Connor in time to save them from the intruder. Something hacked away at the door, something metallic that clanged against the doorknob. It was only a matter of time before the jamb broke and the intruder pushed his way inside to her and Connor.

She planted herself between the doorway and the crib as she looked for a weapon she could use to defend herself and her son. Because whoever this intruder was, however big he was, he wasn't getting to her child—not without one hell of a fight.

Chapter 18

Not wanting to sneak up on Rae's bodyguard, Forrest had called the young officer to let him know he was driving out to her place. But the call went unanswered.

And so did the next one.

And the one after that.

Why the hell wasn't Officer Baker picking up?

Forrest was already pulling into her driveway when the dispatcher's voice emanated from his police radio. "Break-in in progress…"

He didn't even have to hear the address to know that it was Rae's.

"Possible officer down," the dispatcher continued. "He's not responding to radio calls…"

Forrest cursed. He'd known how dangerous the assignment was; he'd been run off the road and injured himself. Guilt weighed heavily on him for putting the young officer in danger and Rae...

He pushed aside thoughts of what could have happened to Rae and Connor. She'd called for help. She was still alive. She had to be.

The call hadn't come in that long ago, and he was here. He stomped on the brakes, slammed the shifter into Park and threw open the door of the SUV. Drawing his weapon from his holster, he headed toward the house. He hurried up the couple of steps to the porch and crossed it to grasp the doorknob with his free hand. It didn't turn; the front door was locked. The intruder hadn't gotten in this way, or if he had, he'd locked the door behind himself.

In his early days of law enforcement, he would have kicked down the door, but if he tried that now, he would mess up all of the rods and pins holding his leg together. Instead he rammed his shoulder against the door over and over until finally the jamb splintered and the dead bolt broke free. He shoved open the door and rushed inside just as a dark figure ran through the kitchen.

"Stop! Police!" he yelled as he raised his weapon. But the man didn't stop. He shoved open the back door and rushed outside.

Forrest couldn't shoot someone in the back, no matter how much he didn't want him getting away. He wanted, even more, to make sure that Rae and Connor were all right, though. Connor's cries rang out, accompanied by Rae's soft, reassuring murmurs.

They were okay. The pressure of guilt eased only

slightly on his chest. He had to check for the officer—
and try to stop the intruder from getting away. Forcing
his leg to move faster, he rushed across the kitchen.
But as he headed out the back door, Rae called after
him, "Don't go!"

He turned back to make sure she was all right.
She stood in the doorway to the nursery, but furniture blocked most of her from view. She'd barricaded
the door.

Of course she had; she would have done anything
to protect her son, whom she was cradling in her arms.

"Don't go!" she said. "He must have hurt the officer."

That was why he needed to go. And she knew it.
"Barricade yourself back inside," he told her. "Other
officers are on their way."

"Then wait!" she said.

He didn't have time to argue, so he just pulled open
the back door and headed off into the night. The officer had to be out here somewhere, but Forrest didn't
call out to him. Instead he just listened.

The silence was all-encompassing—eerily so. If the
intruder was running away, why couldn't Forrest hear
his footsteps against the ground, or the rustle of brush
as he ran from the yard?

He hadn't talked to Rae that long, hadn't given the
intruder that much time to get away. Of course the guy
could move faster than Forrest could. Because of the
damage to his leg, anybody could move faster than he
could. That was why he'd considered it smarter to have
someone else guard Rae and Connor. But he'd put that
officer in danger.

And now he had to find him and help him if he could.

If he wasn't already too late.

Grasping his gun tightly, he moved away from the light on the back patio, toward the shadows. The officer had to be out here somewhere. Officer Baker was too loyal a lawman to have skipped out on security duty.

The crime-scene tape fluttered in the light breeze, drawing Forrest to the area where he'd found the body. And sure enough, he found another body—lying face-down beside that hole. It was nearly as lifeless as the first one he had found. The officer didn't move, murmur or groan.

Forrest hunched down and felt for a pulse in the officer's muscular neck. A faint beat fluttered beneath his fingertips. He was alive. But just barely.

Blood pooled beneath his head from a nasty-looking gash on the back of his skull. Even if he survived, he might never be the same—like Forrest.

Something skittered across the patio stones, something that could have been a shoe scraping across the bricks. Was the intruder hiding somewhere in the shadows, like the shooter had been all of those months ago? Was he waiting to attack when Forrest would least expect it?

Chief Archer Thompson cursed himself as much as he cursed what he'd heard of the dispatcher's call. *Possible officer down...*

Damn it. He should have taken those threats more seriously against Rae Lemmon. Now another officer had probably been hurt protecting her and her baby, just like Forrest Colton had been hurt. Holding his cell phone in his hand, he punched in the contact for Detective Colton. A deep voice answered, but the message was prerecorded, promising a call back when he was available.

Forrest hadn't called in his location, but Archer knew where he was. At Rae Lemmon's.

No matter where he'd been, the detective probably would have made damn certain he was first on the scene.

Archer cursed again. He was good friends with Hays and Josephine Colton. The last thing he ever wanted to do was have to notify them that they'd lost one of their sons—especially on his watch.

His watch?

Hell, he hadn't been watching anything. Consumed with thoughts of how he'd failed his sister, he'd started failing his officers, as well.

As he shoved his phone into his pocket, he pulled out the keys to his SUV. He wouldn't be the first on the scene; he already knew that. But he was going to damn well show up and do whatever he could to save his officers.

And the woman and her baby.

Rae had been terrified when the intruder had been fighting to get inside the nursery. Even though he was gone, she was no less afraid; she just wasn't worried about her and Connor right now. Sirens, ringing out in the distance, announced the imminent arrival of the officers Forrest had said were coming.

But would they get to the house in time to help Forrest? And to help the young officer? Something must have happened to him; he hadn't come back.

Would the intruder?

She shivered as she considered that he might have pulled the same trick on Forrest that he had on the officer. Lure him outside, disable him and then return for her and Connor.

Forrest had told her to barricade herself and Connor back inside the nursery. But as she tried to pull the door closed, it bounced back open against the splintered jamb. The intruder had been determined to get inside—to get to them.

She shuddered as she relived the terror of those moments when the intruder had been so close to them, to hurting her son like his threats had promised. But then Forrest had rushed to her rescue—again.

At risk of endangering his own life.

He wasn't rushing back inside. Was it because he was busy helping the officer?

Or had something happened to him?

Fear had her heart pounding frantically, and Connor, clasped in her arms, must have felt that fear, as he continued to scream despite her efforts to comfort him. But she struggled to comfort Connor, because she needed comfort so badly herself.

But only one person could offer her that: Forrest.

She needed him to come back to her. She needed him to be safe and unhurt.

Each minute he stayed outside dragged on and on and increased her fear. If not for Connor, she would have gone outside to look for Forrest—to make certain he was all right. But she couldn't put the baby in danger.

Why was he in danger?

What did the intruder want from her? She couldn't stop the murder investigation. She couldn't stop Forrest from doing his job.

But the intruder could.

And maybe he had.

Where the hell was Forrest?

She heard footsteps against the hardwood as someone came in through the front door. But no voice called out to her. It wasn't him.

He'd gone out the back, so he wouldn't have come in the front. But the intruder might have—if he'd circled around the house to come back for her and Connor.

Using her hip, she shoved the dresser back against the battered door to the nursery. It hadn't kept the intruder out last time, though.

And she doubted it would keep him out any longer this time.

Chapter 19

The ambulance tore out of the driveway, lights flashing and sirens blaring. The chief had climbed into the back with the young officer. Two police vehicles drove in front of it and one behind to escort the fallen officer safely to the hospital.

Officer Baker had regained consciousness while Forrest had been checking his pulse. Baker's first concern had been for Rae and Connor, though, not for himself.

He was a good cop. And since he'd been so lucid, Forrest was fairly confident that he'd be all right. He'd been tempted to climb into the ambulance, along with the chief, and make sure the officer arrived at the hospital. But the cop wasn't the only one in danger.

Rae and Connor were also in danger, since the intruder had tried so hard to get to them again.

What had he intended to do to them?

Hurt them?

Kill them?

Killing them wouldn't get Forrest to back off from finding the killer. It would make him so much more determined to stop the guy so that he wouldn't be able to hurt anyone else. Ever.

So, was it the killer?

Or was it someone else?

Someone who might have cased the situation earlier that day when he'd come to visit her.

After watching the ambulance disappear from sight, Forrest walked back into the house. He wasn't the only member of law enforcement who'd stayed behind. In addition to the officers fixing the locks and the broken window of the kitchen door, there was a whole crew of techs in the backyard, looking for evidence from the officer's attack. A few other officers searched the property for the intruder. If he was here, they would find him.

But Forrest was pretty damn certain he'd gotten away. Again.

If only he'd moved faster—if only he'd been *able* to move faster—he might have caught the son of a bitch before he'd even gotten out of the house. He knew he should appoint one of the other officers to protect Connor and Rae. But an image of burly Officer Baker, bleeding and unconscious, burned in his mind.

Forrest didn't want to put anyone else in danger.

But he sure as hell didn't want Rae and Connor in danger either.

She pulled the nursery door shut behind her and joined him in the living room. "Is Officer Baker going to be all right?" she asked anxiously.

He lifted his shoulders in a slight shrug. "I don't know for certain, but he had regained consciousness and was lucid when I found him."

She expelled a little ragged sigh. "That's a good sign then."

It didn't mean he was out of danger, though.

Neither was she.

Yet.

"You need to pack up some stuff for you and Connor," he said. "We need to get you out of here." He should have made her leave the house when he'd first found that body in her backyard—then she wouldn't have been threatened at all.

But the intruder had left a note at her office, too.

Maybe it wouldn't matter where she went; she would still be in danger.

She shook her head. "No. I just finally got Connor settled down again. I don't want to risk waking him up."

"But you're not safe here," Forrest said. "Surely you realize that now."

"I wasn't safe with one officer," she said. But she gestured at him and at the officers who were finishing up with the locks. "But there are more than one here now."

"Not for much longer," Forrest said.

"We're actually done now," one of the young cops chimed into the conversation.

Forrest nodded his permission. "You can leave now."

While they left, Rae stared at him with narrowed eyes.

"They want to get to the hospital to check on their friend," he told her.

She flinched. "Of course. I'm sorry. You probably want to do that, too."

"I'm not leaving you here," he said. "You need to come with me."

"Where?" she asked, and her fear cracked her voice when she added, "Where will Connor and I be safe?"

"With me," he said.

"Then stay," she said. "Stay with me."

It was selfish. Rae knew it the moment the words had left her lips. She was putting him in danger again. But the break-in had scared her so badly that she didn't care how selfish she was being. She just wanted to feel safe again, and she only felt safe with Forrest.

"I'm not leaving," Forrest said, "without you."

"I'm not going anywhere tonight," she said. "Connor has already been through enough."

"And if the intruder returns?" Forrest asked.

She gestured at the backyard, which was aglow with lights from the crime-scene technicians. "He might have been brave enough to take on one police officer—but a whole yard of them?" She shook her head. "He's not that…"

What was he?

Why was he so determined to hurt her or Connor? Or was he trying to hurt Forrest?

The best thing she could do for Forrest was to send him away. But he was the only one who really made her feel safe—when she was in his arms. She didn't want him to leave, but she didn't want him winding up in an ambulance. Again.

"We don't know what he is," Forrest finished for her. "Or do you know now? Did you see him?" He stepped closer to her and wrapped his big hands around her arms.

She could feel the strength in those hands and the heat of his touch through the thin material of her summer robe. Her skin tingled, and awareness and desire coursed through her. She shook her head, as much in denial of those feelings as in response to his question.

"But he'd broken open the nursery door," Forrest said, almost as if he doubted her.

"I didn't see him," she said. "I just saw the nursery door being pushed in—along with the furniture I'd stacked behind it—after he broke the lock on it."

"How do you know it's a man then?" he asked.

She opened her mouth then closed it again, pausing to think before replying. "I don't know. I just assumed since he hurt the officer and broke down the door..." Heat rushed to her face with embarrassment that she would be so sexist. "But that doesn't mean that a woman couldn't have done that, as well."

"She could have," Forrest agreed. "You stacked all that furniture against the nursery door."

"To protect my son," she said.

He nodded. "I've seen the strength a mother can summon when her child is in danger."

She didn't know if he was referring to something he'd witnessed while working in Austin or as a volunteer with the Cowboy Heroes or...

He slid his hands up to her biceps and gently squeezed. And she knew; he was talking about her. "You're amazing."

She shrugged. "I'm not so sure about that. I don't know what I would have done if you hadn't showed up when you did."

"You would have fought him off as long as you could," he said, flinching as if the thought brought him pain.

"Him?" she questioned. "Did you see him when you rushed in?"

"Not his face," he said. "But from his build, I believe the intruder was male."

He sounded like a cop. He also sounded as if he was keeping something from her. He might not have seen the guy's face, but he might have recognized something else about him.

"Do you have some idea who it is?" she asked.

"I am looking into leads," he said.

"Who?" she asked.

"Is it just a coincidence that the intruder breaks in after your boss visited today?"

"Boss?" she asked, struggling to focus. Maybe it was because his hands were still on her arms, almost stroking her muscles now. Maybe it was because she wasn't sure what he was talking about. "What...? Oh, Kenneth. He's not actually my boss." Which was good because she probably would have had to quit now.

As it was, she wasn't sure how to handle that situation. If she reported him, would anyone believe that he'd stepped out of line with her? Had he? Or was he just naturally kind of creepy?

"What is he?" Forrest asked, his voice suddenly very gruff, and his deep-set hazel eyes were intense as he stared down at her.

"A colleague," she said. "Sometimes I work on his cases, but not very often, and he never assigns the work to me."

"Then why was he here today?" Forrest asked as he continued to stare at her with such intensity, it almost made her think that he was jealous.

Over her?

Did she mean more to him than an assignment, than someone to protect?

"Why do you care?" she wondered aloud.

"I'm investigating murders and those threats," he said, "so I need to know everything I can about possible suspects, about someone who might have had access to your backyard."

She pointed out the kitchen window, but the lights had gone out now. The technicians must have finished processing the scene. "I would say anyone, but…"

He glanced out the window, too.

And she shivered. "They're gone now."

"The techs, yeah," he said. "But I have a unit posted at the end of your driveway, and another officer will remain in the backyard." He glanced out the kitchen door, his brow furrowing with concern. Clearly he felt as bad as she did that the officer had been harmed protecting her.

"I hope he'll be all right," she said.

He nodded. "Me, too."

The wounded officer wasn't her only concern,

though. She didn't want Forrest getting hurt, as well. "With all that protection, I don't need you to stay here, too," she said. "You can go home."

He shook his head. "No, I can't."

"But you said there are other officers—"

He leaned down and brushed his mouth across hers. "I can't leave you," he said.

Relief and desire rushed through her, and she reached out, winding her arms around his lean waist. She wanted to hang on to him for comfort, for pleasure—forever.

But she knew better than to plan on anyone sticking around forever. So she would just make herself be happy with another night with Forrest. Keeping her arms around him, she walked backward toward her bedroom, tugging him along with her.

He stumbled a bit, and she worried that he'd hurt his leg. But then he reached down and lifted her into his arms and carried her toward her bedroom. So there was nothing wrong with his leg; he was just as impatient to be together again as she was. After shouldering open her bedroom door, he pressed it closed the same way and carried her to the bed across which law books were strewn.

"Always working," he murmured, and he stared down at her with something like awe on his handsome face.

"So are you," she said.

Dark circles rimmed his beautiful eyes, and she knew he'd given up sleep to work his cases. And now he was giving up more sleep to be with her.

He shook his head. "It isn't work being with you. It's pleasure."

That was what he gave to her…when he peeled off her robe and her T-shirt. He pressed his lips to every inch of her body, kissing and teasing with his tongue until she quivered from the ecstasy gripping her body.

He made love to her thoroughly before he even took off his own clothes. Then she kissed every inch of skin he exposed, every muscle, every scar.

She made love to him with her mouth, and with her entire heart—because it was his. He just didn't know it, and she didn't want him to know. She didn't want to be disappointed.

But physically he didn't disappoint. He teased her nipples into taut peaks and made her throb and squirm with the tension that built inside her. Then finally he sheathed himself in a condom, and he filled her.

He filled that hollow place inside her. He completed her, and she clutched at him, matching his frantic rhythm until finally they came—together. The power of their climax rocked and humbled Rae. She'd never felt so much ever—even with him.

The words burned in her throat, the love she felt for him. But maybe it was just the passion. So she held the words inside even as the feeling overwhelmed her. As he overwhelmed her.

"Can't you do anything right?" the voice on the phone asked him.

He flinched at the question—flinched because he

already knew the answer. No. He couldn't do anything right. He never had.

Whenever he'd tried, he usually only made a bigger mess of things. Of his life and everyone else's.

That was why it was better when he was gone— for all those left behind, but he couldn't leave yet. He couldn't leave with the debt being held over his head right now.

"I don't know what you mean," he lied.

But the caller—whoever the hell he was—snorted in disbelief. "Yeah, right. You screwed up again and you damn well know it."

How did *he* know? Who was he? Did he have eyes and ears everywhere?

Maybe his wasn't the only debt this guy had bought. Or maybe he had other means to control and manipulate other people.

"How did I screw up?" he asked. "No cop is working the murder cases right now. Everybody's trying to figure out who hurt the cop."

Such a long pause followed his pronouncement that he would have thought the caller had hung up on him if not for his cell screen showing that the unknown number was still connected to his. He hadn't answered it the first time the number had called his, but then the notes had started appearing under the door of his motel room.

The threats.

"If just a cop getting hurt distracted the Whisperwood PD this much, then what will happen when you kill one?" the caller questioned.

"You want me to kill a cop." It wasn't a question. He knew this guy—whoever he was—wasn't playing.

"The cop or your kid—you choose."

There was no choice. He'd already cost his kid too damn much to cost her anything else.

Chapter 20

What the hell was wrong with him? Why couldn't he keep his hands off Rae Lemmon? It wasn't just his hands he needed to keep off her, though. It was his lips and his body and his…

Forrest swallowed the groan burning his throat and resisted—just barely—the urge to turn around and go back to Rae's bedroom, back to Rae. He still wanted her so badly. But giving in to that desire—again—had been a mistake.

He was supposed to be protecting her and Connor, and he wasn't doing a very damn good job when he kept letting desire distract him from his duty. He pushed open the broken door to the nursery and crossed the room to the crib.

The baby slept peacefully; his little rosebud lips

parted on a soft sigh. His face was flushed, either from the ordeal he'd been through earlier that evening or from the heat in the room.

The air-conditioning unit either wasn't big enough to cool off the ranch house that much, or it was old and needed repairs. It just cut the heat and humidity a little bit, but not enough to really cool off the house, though. The night air might have been cooler than the faint trickle of air emanating from the ducts, but it was too risky to open windows.

Too risky with the intruder determined to get to Connor and Rae.

But why?

What could they have to do with the murder investigation—besides the fact that a body had been found in their backyard? Not that it had been all that accidentally found, like Jonah and Maggie had found the body of the chief's long-missing sister.

Forrest was pretty damn sure the body he'd found had been purposely dug up. Why? And who would know it had been there besides the killer?

"Do you know, Connor?" he asked the baby as he reached into the crib and ran his hand over the infant's soft hair. His blood heated with the memory of someone snipping off a lock of that hair to leave on Rae's pillow with the note.

His gut clenched with anger and guilt that she'd had to go through that, that someone was putting her through a mother's worst nightmare—someone threatening her child.

His hand trembled a little against Connor's head,

and another little sigh slipped out of the baby's mouth. Not wanting to frighten him any more than he'd already been that night, Forrest pulled his hand away.

He had to make sure that Connor didn't get scared again. He had to make sure that the baby and the baby's mother stayed safe. As he left the nursery, he pulled the door as closed as it could get in the broken jamb and headed into the kitchen. He took out his cell phone and connected himself with the unit guarding the driveway at the street.

"This is Detective Colton. Is everything all right?"

"Except for the chief picking up his vehicle a while ago, there has been no sign of anyone else on the property, sir," the officer replied.

Heat rushed to Forrest's face. The chief had been here while he'd been distracted with Rae. Had he looked into the house? Had he seen that Forrest hadn't been protecting them like he'd promised?

Then the other reason for the chief leaving the hospital sunk into Forrest, and a twinge of guilt struck his heart. "Is Officer Baker all right?" he asked. The chief wouldn't have left him if he wasn't—unless there'd been nothing more for him to do.

"He has a concussion and skull fracture and will have to stay a couple of days in the hospital, but the doctor told the chief and Officer Baker's family that he should be just fine."

Forrest uttered a heavy sigh of relief. "That's great."

He should have checked on him sooner for himself. But he could barely think when he was close to Rae. And when he was touching her, he couldn't think at all.

That was why he needed to stay away from her. "What about the officer posted in the backyard?" he asked as he peered out the door, into the night. "Where's he?"

"Backyard?"

"At the crime scene."

"He left with the technicians," the officer replied. "He thought he was only supposed to guard them while they were working."

Forrest swallowed a curse. He was such a damn fool with Rae's and Connor's safety.

Despite his efforts to muffle his oath, the officer must have heard it. "Really, sir, we haven't seen anyone lurking around the property, and with the exception of the chief, nobody has come and gone."

But what if the intruder had still been somewhere on the property? What if he'd hidden somewhere and the officers at the scene hadn't found him?

Then he could be somewhere close—too close for Forrest's comfort. He reached for his holster and drew his gun from it. "I think I'll walk around the house myself, just to make sure everything's okay."

"Sir, one of us can come up and do that for you," the officer offered.

"No," he said. "I could use the air." The air to clear his head, and the distance from Rae so that he could stop being so damn distracted with how he felt about her.

With how much he felt for her. Too damn much.

"After what happened to Officer Baker, are you sure it's safe?" the officer asked.

"You said nobody's come and gone," Forrest reminded the officer. "So it should be safe."

But despite the warmth in the house, a chill raced down his spine, raising goose bumps on his skin. And he knew...

The threat was still here—still too damn close to Connor and Rae. Forrest needed to find it and remove it.

"Do you want us to check in with you at a certain time and make sure everything's okay at the house?" the officer asked.

"Yes," Forrest agreed. That way, if his suspicion was right, there would be protection for Rae. "And if you don't hear from me, come up right away," he advised. "Or if you hear anything suspicious."

Like his gun firing.

He wouldn't mind shooting the son of a bitch who'd been terrorizing Rae and Connor. He wouldn't mind at all.

"Will do, Detective," the officer replied. "But I'm sure we'll be hearing from you soon."

He hoped. But that chill chased down his spine again. He clicked off the cell and reached for the handle of the back door. Maybe he should have woken up Rae to let her know he was going outside. But he didn't want to worry her if there was no reason for his concern.

After all, the officers at the driveway hadn't seen anyone coming and going but the chief. And the chief must not have seen anyone either. So really, maybe the fear

Forrest felt had nothing to do with something outside and everything to do with what was inside the house.

Rae.

Connor.

And his feelings for them.

If he went back into the bedroom, he wouldn't just wake up Rae. He would slide into that bed with her, take her in his arms and make love to her all over again.

His body tensed just thinking about it, about her and how damn much he wanted her. But giving in to that desire he felt for her was a betrayal of the promise he'd made to protect her and Connor. And too many people had already broken their promises to Rae.

He didn't want to be the next man to let her down. So he drew in a breath, unlocked the door and pulled it open. After pulling it closed behind him, he drew the extra key to the new lock from his pocket and turned the dead bolt. Shoving the key back into his pocket, he turned around and peered into the shadows.

The moon hung low in the sky, illuminating much of the dark, but for the shadows near the mounds of dirt around the old grave site. Who was the victim and why had she been buried here, on Rae Lemmon's property?

Forrest had found out easily enough who Patrice Eccleston was, but the identity of this body was so far eluding everyone. She'd been dead for a long time, though—probably as long as the chief's sister had been.

Had this woman's family thought—like the chief's

had—that she'd just run away? Was there not even a missing-person report on her?

Maybe that was why he couldn't find her—because nobody had missed her. Drawn by thoughts of the mummified corpse, he crossed the yard to the crime-scene tape that fluttered from the poles stabbed into the ground around the hole. More tape had been strewn around another area near the hole, where the officer had been struck. He would be okay, though.

Forrest breathed a sigh of relief for that. He hadn't wanted to put anyone else in danger, but he sure as hell didn't want Rae and Connor in danger either. Why were they? Who would threaten them?

He glanced back at the house, and from the corner of his eye, he noticed some movement behind him. He slid off the safety as he turned, but before he could squeeze the trigger, something swung out of the shadows at him. Metal struck his head right by his temple, and everything immediately went black.

His legs buckled beneath him and he dropped to the ground. And as he did, his last thought was that he'd failed Rae. He'd broken that promise to her.

Seconds before now he'd stared down a gun barrel; now he stared down at the man who'd held that gun on him. Detective Colton had good reflexes. He was lucky he hadn't taken a bullet. But fortunately he'd moved faster.

Now Colton wasn't moving at all. He tightened his grasp on the pipe and considered swinging it again. If he killed him—like the caller wanted—maybe this would end now. Maybe the caller would consider his debt paid in full.

He'd struck the younger cop harder and hadn't killed him, though. So he dropped the pipe and leaned down to pick up the gun instead.

If he wanted to make sure Forrest Colton died, he needed to shoot him. Needed to make sure there was no way he would survive.

But when he tugged on the gun, he couldn't get it loose from Colton's grasp. The man was unconscious, but he still held tightly to his weapon. The only way to stop a guy like Colton was to kill him.

Rae jerked awake, her body nearly convulsing with the strange feeling that had passed through her. She reached out for Forrest, but her fingers slid across tangled sheets. He was gone.

Again.

Every time they'd made love, he'd left her afterward. Was he trying to make it clear to her that he didn't want to stay? She wouldn't have expected him to; she never expected anyone to stay.

But why had she awakened like she had?

She reached for the baby monitor next to the bed and listened for Connor's cry. Maybe that was what had awakened her. The baby was quiet.

But a strange noise did emanate from the speaker, a strange squeak of the floorboards, as if someone was walking around the floor of the nursery.

A smile curved her lips.

That was where Forrest had gone—to check on Connor. That was where she had found him those other times, leaning over the crib, staring at her beautiful son. She'd even caught him singing that one night.

She waited for him to sing again, but he wouldn't want to wake Connor. He only wanted to protect him.

Like he only wanted to protect her.

She was the one who wanted more—despite knowing better, despite knowing that she was just like her mother. Just like beautiful Georgia, Rae had a habit of picking men who couldn't do permanence.

Only temporary.

Like Forrest was only temporarily working with the Whisperwood Police Department. Once the killer was caught, he would leave. Either return to Austin or continue volunteering with the Cowboy Heroes, going wherever they were sent.

But he was here now.

With her son.

Rae crawled out of bed and pulled on her T-shirt and her robe. She needed to protect herself from Forrest, from her feelings for him. But despite the couple of layers of fabric, she still felt naked, like he could see straight through everything, right to her heart.

She loved him.

And if she found him holding Connor as gently as he had in the past, she knew he would see that love on her face. Maybe she should just stay in bed, pretending to sleep, so that he wouldn't know how much he meant to her.

But now a cry emanated from the speaker. Connor

had awakened, but the voice that murmured something to him wasn't Forrest's.

She froze with fear for just a second before she rushed from her room. Would she get to the nursery in time to save her son?

And what had happened to Forrest?

Chapter 21

Pain throbbed at his temple, pounding at Forrest to wake up. But it wasn't just the pain hammering at him; his heart pounded with fear. He'd left Rae and Connor unprotected. After dragging his eyes open, he blinked away the blackness. Then he pushed his way up from the ground. The gun was in his hand yet. The intruder hadn't wrested it away from him. But his pocket had been turned inside out, and the key was gone.

Cursing, Forrest ran toward the house. His leg throbbed like his head, but he ignored the pain as he pushed himself. The back door stood open, like the intruder had been in a hurry to get inside. So was Forrest.

He didn't even take time to call out to the unit at the road. They would be checking in soon enough, since he hadn't called them. But he didn't want to waste a moment in getting to Rae and Connor.

Then her scream rang out. And he knew he was already too late. She stood in the doorway to the nursery, with a hand clasped over her mouth as if she wanted to take back her scream.

Connor echoed it as he cried out.

He was alive.

They were both alive.

But they were clearly in danger. Forrest rushed up behind Rae and then pulled her away from the door. Shielding her with his body, he burst into the nursery.

A man held the screaming baby even more awkwardly than Forrest had held him. But maybe that was because he didn't just hold the baby; he also held a pipe that was smeared with blood. Forrest's blood probably. Some trailed from his temple, down the side of his face.

And Officer Baker's…

Forrest cursed and tightened his grasp on his gun. "Put the baby back in the crib," he said. "Right now." He stared down the barrel at the man's face, which looked vaguely familiar. Where the hell had he seen him before?

It didn't matter now, though. Nothing mattered but saving Connor. Would he be hurt if Forrest shot the man?

Rae must have thought so, because she grabbed Forrest's arm and pleaded, "Don't shoot."

Forrest wanted to protect the baby, too, desperately— almost as if he was Connor's father. "Put him down," he ordered the man. "Put him down or I will shoot you."

"Don't," Rae pleaded again. "He's my dad."

That was why he'd looked vaguely familiar. Years had passed—hard years—since the photographs Forrest had seen in the old album had been taken, but he had the same bone structure beneath the wrinkles and dark circles. He was even leaner than he'd been then, and a hell of a lot more desperate-looking.

So desperate that Forrest still didn't trust him with the baby. Even knowing now that he was Connor's grandfather, Forrest believed he still might hurt the baby. To hurt Rae?

Hadn't he already hurt her enough?

"Put down the baby," Forrest said again as he kept the gun barrel trained on the man.

"I'm not going to hurt him," Beau Lemmon said, as if he'd read Forrest's mind or maybe the fear on his face.

"Just like you didn't hurt me or Officer Baker with that damn pipe you're holding?" he asked.

Rae gasped, and her fingers slipped from Forrest's arm. She must have just realized what her father was, the one who'd been threatening her all this time.

The one who'd already tried once to kill Forrest before trying again tonight.

Rae hadn't been able to look away from her father since first finding him in the nursery, holding his grandson. But now she looked at Forrest, at the blood running down the side of his face. Her father had done that?

And he'd hurt the young officer, as well?

And had driven Forrest off the road, with Connor in the back seat?

She'd been angry with her father for years for leaving her mother and her. But what rushed through her now was so much more than anger. It was hot and vicious and a rage that nearly blinded her with its intensity. She edged around Forrest and rushed across the nursery.

"Don't you dare touch him!" she yelled at her father as she reached for her son.

He released him into her arms. Not that she would have given him a choice. She didn't want him touching her baby. Ever. But especially not now, with that pipe in his hand.

"What were you going to do to him?" she asked, her heart cracking with fear. "Were you going to kill my child? Your grandchild? What kind of monster are you?"

"A dangerous one," Forrest answered for him as he stepped between them again, using his body—his already battered body—to shield her and her baby.

Her father could have killed him. He'd nearly killed the cop.

Her father...

Her stomach churned with the realization. And she'd been upset when he'd deserted her and her mother.

Obviously they'd been better off—and safer—without him in their lives.

"Get out!" she told him. "Get out of here. Now!"

"He can't leave," Forrest corrected her. "Not on his

own. He needs to go to jail." And he began reading him his rights.

But her father didn't take his advice; he didn't remain silent. "No. You don't understand. You're in danger. You're all in danger."

Forrest snorted. "Yeah, from you." And with his free hand, he reached for the bloody pipe. "Your fingerprints are going to be all over this. And if you hadn't burned the van you stole to run me and Connor off the road, your fingerprints would have been all over that, too. You're going to jail."

"Then you won't catch the killer," Beau said. "And nobody will be safe until he's caught."

Forrest, standing between them, tensed.

"You have to get Rae and the baby out of here," Beau continued. "They're not safe here. Once I'm in jail, he'll just send someone else after them. After you…" He glanced around as if he could hear them coming. "Or he'll take care of you himself—just like he did those women."

"Who is it?" Forrest asked, but he sounded skeptical, as if he was just humoring her father.

Beau shook his head. "I don't know."

Forrest snorted and then continued reading him the Miranda rights.

Beau held up his hands. "I'm telling the truth. He bought out my gambling debts. He owns me. That's why I was—"

"Terrifying your own daughter?" Forrest finished for him.

"I was trying to save her," Beau said. "Trying to warn her."

"With threats?" Forrest asked.

"Those weren't for her," Beau said. "They were for me. Whoever this killer is—he sent me the notes, threatening my kid. Threatening Rae."

Anger coursed through her again. "You're the one who threatened me. Who broke in here—"

"Into my own house?" he asked. "That's not breaking and entering."

"It's not your house," she corrected him. "Mom left it to me. Do you even know she's gone? That the cancer came back? Do you even care?" She didn't know why she asked; it was clear that he didn't, or he never would have left. Her mother had deserved better. *She* deserved better. "Get him out of here," she told Forrest.

But the detective hesitated. "How did the person get these notes to you? How do you not know who the killer is?"

Beau pushed a hand through his thin gray hair. "I found the notes under my motel-room door, and the calls came from an unknown number."

"Did you recognize the voice?" Forrest asked.

He shook his head.

"Why are you talking to him?" Rae asked. She just wanted the man gone, like he'd been for all of these years, when she'd actually needed him.

She didn't need him now.

And she would make sure she never needed anyone else. But Connor…

She rocked the crying baby in her arms. He was all she needed.

"He could have killed me," Forrest said. "After he knocked me out, he could have finished me off. He could have finished off Officer Baker, too."

He didn't think her father was a killer. The pressure on her heart eased slightly. She didn't want to believe he was a killer either. She didn't want to believe that she and Connor had that in their DNA.

But…

"The body that was buried in the backyard…" she murmured. "Who was she?"

Her father shook his head. "I don't know."

"But you dug it up," Forrest guessed.

"I knew it was there," he admitted.

Rae shuddered. She'd grown up in this house, played in that yard, and her father had allowed it all, knowing that a corpse had been buried there.

"We'll talk more once I get you down to lockup," Forrest said. Maybe he wanted to spare her the gory details.

But she didn't need his protection from the truth. Just from danger.

"If you lock me up, I won't be able to help you," Beau said. "And she won't be safe until the killer is caught."

"You don't know who it is," Forrest reminded him. "So you can't help me."

"I can find out," Beau offered. "I can bring him to you."

Forrest shook his head. "You think I'm going to trust you?"

"You want to keep them safe, too," Beau said. "You know that's not possible until the killer is caught."

"Stop using me!" Rae said. "You've never given a damn about me or about my mother. Why are you pretending to care now?"

"I always cared," Beau said. "That's why I left. I was more a hindrance than a help to both of you. Georgia deserved better, and so do you." He looked at Forrest now, as if he was wondering if Forrest was worthy of her. "If you care about her at all, you'd get her the hell out of here. You'd do whatever was necessary to keep her and the baby safe—even trust me."

She reached out and touched Forrest's arm again, but not to pull down the gun he was pointing at her father. "Don't," she advised. "Don't trust him."

And just as she said it, her father pounced. He pulled the pipe from Forrest's hand and swung it at his head. A gun went off, the blast deafening.

Connor, who had been crying, suddenly stopped. Was he just in shock? Or had he been hit?

With the adrenaline coursing through Rae, she might have been hit, too, and just didn't realize it yet. She had no idea what was going on—as wood cracked and glass broke—and the room exploded with people and chaos.

She just held her son closely, using her body to shield his as Forrest had the two of them. If anyone had been hit, it would have been Forrest.

He had already been hurt, bleeding, wounded…

Because of her father.

All of the years she'd spent wishing he would come back haunted her now. She would have been happier and safer had she never seen him again.

And what about Forrest?

Was he all right?

Chapter 22

How the hell had he gotten away?

Forrest's arm ached from where the pipe had struck him, but ignoring the pain, he tightened his grasp on the steering wheel.

If only he hadn't let Rae distract him.

But it hadn't been just Rae. An engine roaring down the driveway had drawn his attention away from Beau Lemmon, as well. All that talk of her still being in danger. Of another killer.

Forrest thought that whoever was coming was a threat, not his backup. But it had been the other officers who'd broken down the front door and burst into the house.

By the time they'd arrived, it had already been too late. Beau Lemmon had gotten away. After striking him with the pipe and making the gun go off, the older man had hurled himself out the nursery window.

Forrest cursed himself for not slapping cuffs immediately on the guy's wrists and taking him off to jail. But what he'd been saying…

It had made sense.

"You really think there's someone else?" Rae asked. "That he's not the killer?"

He glanced across the console to where she sat in the passenger's seat, with her arms wrapped around herself as if that was all that held her together. She looked at him with a faint flicker of hope in her dark eyes.

She needed to believe this.

Needed to believe in something.

"If he was a killer, I would be dead," Forrest said. His head and arm hurt damn badly, though, but she didn't need to know that.

She needed to know her father wasn't the monster she'd accused him of being.

"But he drove you off the road and hit you over the head," she reminded him. Needlessly.

Forrest wasn't about to forget or forgive what Beau Lemmon had done to him and the young officer. "But I think he was acting on someone else's orders," Forrest admitted. "Just like he said."

"That someone bought out his debt and was using it to control him?" she asked, with skepticism in her soft voice.

She deserved to know the truth. "I checked into your father," Forrest said. "And he's done some desperate things in the past to pay back his debts."

She gasped. "Murder?"

"No," he said. "Petty stuff. Breaking and entering. Stealing."

"That might be petty to you," she said. "But not to me. And his hurting people…" She reached across the console then and brushed her fingertips over the lump on his forearm. "Are you okay?"

He glanced at her again, at her face as she peered up at him, at the wound on his temple. She was so damn beautiful—even with as upset as she was.

"I'm fine," he said, not wanting her to worry about him. He was worried, though. And he kept glancing into the rearview mirror. He had a police escort in front of him and another behind, but he wasn't sure if that was a good idea. He might have been better able to spot and lose a tailing vehicle on his own.

Not that he'd lost Beau Lemmon that day he'd dropped Rae at work. Beau was damn good at following. Was he behind them now? Or was he doing what he'd promised? Was he trying to find out the identity of the killer?

Maybe that was why Forrest hadn't gone out the window after him. Of course he'd had to make sure that the people breaking into the house weren't a threat to Rae and Connor. But once they'd identified themselves, he hadn't chased after Beau as fast as he could have.

Despite all of the years the man had been gone, he knew the property well. So well that he must have had a place on it where he could hide from them.

That was why Forrest had insisted Rae pack up Connor and leave. And this time, staring at the broken window and the splintered doorjamb of her son's room, she had just nodded in agreement. Connor slept in his carrier in the back seat, with a couple bags next to him.

"Are you okay?" he asked Rae.

She jerked her head in a sharp nod. "I told you I didn't get hurt."

After the gun had gone off, she and Connor had seemed to go into shock. The blast had been loud, though.

He flinched, regretting that he hadn't put the safety back on, but he hadn't trusted her father. And with good reason.

Over the course of his career, Forrest had met a lot of desperate people, but Beau Lemmon might have been the most desperate of them all. As desperate as he was, though, he hadn't killed.

Yet.

It was hard to say if he could be driven to it, though. For Rae—to keep her safe—he might have actually done it.

"I'm not talking about physically," Forrest said.

She uttered a ragged-sounding sigh. "It was a shock to see him again."

Especially the way she'd seen him—in the nursery, holding her son and a bloody pipe. Maybe the image had played through her mind again, because she shuddered.

"He's long gone now," she murmured.

"I'll find him," Forrest assured her.

"To put him in jail," she said.

He couldn't tell if that upset her or not. "Don't you want me to arrest him?"

"Jail might be the safest place for him," she admitted. "It might save him from himself."

"Gambling is an addiction," he said.

She sucked in a breath, drawing his attention back to her. She stared at him, her brown eyes wide and warm with...

Something he didn't dare name, something he didn't dare hope he saw. But he found himself asking, "What?"

"I can't believe you're defending him," she said, "after everything he's done to you."

"For you," he reminded her. "He was trying to protect you."

She sighed. "You give him more credit than I do. Beau Lemmon has always been most concerned with himself, more so than anyone else."

He flinched over the pang of guilt striking him. He'd had no idea how damn lucky he was to have the loving, supportive parents he had. "I'm sorry," he murmured.

"I had my mom," Rae said. "And she more than made up for Beau Lemmon."

But her mom was gone, leaving Rae all alone, but for Connor and her friends. She cared so much for her friends that she'd refused to put them in danger. She hadn't wanted to come here either, but he'd convinced her it would be safe.

And he pulled the SUV through the gates of the Colton ranch. He'd brought her and Connor home with him.

* * *

Rae hesitated before stepping out of the door he'd opened for her. "Are you sure this is a good idea?" she asked as she glanced over at the big farmhouse. Despite the late hour, lights glowed in several of the windows.

"You'll be safe here," Forrest assured her.

"But what about them?" she asked. "I don't want to put your parents in danger." Like her parent had put her in danger with his damn gambling debts.

If she believed him, that is.

If he wasn't actually the killer…

Where her father was concerned, she had no idea what to believe. The only man she wanted to believe now was Forrest. She wanted to trust that he would keep his promise to keep her and Connor safe.

But she didn't want him putting his own life or the lives of his family at risk to do that.

"My parents are happy to have you both here," Forrest assured her.

And he must have been telling the truth because the front door opened and the older Coltons stepped onto the porch. His father wore a plaid robe over his pajamas, and his mother wore a pale pink one. Her white hair glowed in the light spilling out of the house.

"Thank goodness you're here," his mother called out to them. "We've been so concerned."

About their son—of course. He'd already been hurt once protecting her, and now again.

They must hate her or at least resent her.

But when Forrest led her up the steps to the porch, with the carrier dangling from one of his hands, his mother reached out. She closed her arms around Rae and hugged her. "You poor girl," she said. "You've been through so much."

Warmth flooded Rae. From her years managing the general store, Rae knew the Coltons. They had always been friendly to her. But this—opening their home to her and Connor—was beyond friendly.

"You're sure about this?" Rae asked. "Sure that you want us here?" She peered over Mrs. Colton's shoulder at her husband's serious face.

Hays had a face that was hard to read, as his expression was carefully guarded. He studied her for several long moments before a smile curved his lips. "Of course we do, Rae. Of course we do."

The rancher had a reputation for being an honest man, so she wanted to trust him. But she wasn't sure if they had extended their hospitality for her sake or for their son's. Mrs. Colton pulled back now and turned toward her son. She touched the side of his face where the blood had dried.

"Are you okay?" she asked, her soft voice cracking with concern.

He smiled at his mother. "Of course I am. Think of all the times you and Dad called me hardheaded."

"Too many to count," Hays murmured.

Forrest chuckled.

His mother closed her arms around him, hugging him as tightly as she had Rae. Then she pulled back and peered down at the carrier Forrest had in his hand.

"Oh, my…" She sighed. "He's just beautiful. Beautiful."

Pride swelled Rae's heart. He was the reason she was here—that she had agreed to impose on Forrest's parents. She would do anything for Connor.

Just as it was clear that the Coltons would do anything for their son—even put themselves in danger.

"Let's get you all inside," Josephine Colton said as she pulled open the door to the house. "I've already freshened up the nursery for Bellamy and Donovan's baby, so it's all ready for Connor."

That warmth in Rae's heart spread even more. Her best friend was so lucky to have this woman as her mother-in-law. It would be months before Bellamy's baby was here, but Josephine was already eagerly anticipating and preparing for her grandbaby. And even though Donovan wasn't biologically their child, they had always treated him like he was a Colton. So they would treat his child the same way.

But why would they extend their hospitality to Rae and Connor?

Was it because she was Bellamy's friend? Or did they know that something was going on between her and their son? Had Forrest told them...

What?

That they were sleeping together? Well, she was the only one who slept. He didn't. He made love to her and left. Now that warmth spread to her face as embarrassment overwhelmed her.

What had Forrest told his parents?

"Don't worry," Hays told her as he closed and locked the front door behind them.

Forrest and his mother had already headed toward

the stairwell that led up to the second story. But Hays hung back to assure her. "You're safe here—you and your boy." He reached out and touched her cheek. "And you're also very welcome to be here."

Tears stung her eyes.

Why couldn't Beau Lemmon have been half the man that Hays Colton was?

Choked with emotion, she couldn't verbally express her gratitude. So she hugged him.

He froze for a moment before gently patting her back. "You've been on your own entirely too long, young lady."

She blinked away the tears and pulled back. "I'm fine. I have my friends and now my son." When she looked for him, being carried up the stairs by Forrest, her gaze focused on the man instead of the baby, though.

She wanted more. She wanted Forrest.

She wanted a love like his parents had—a marriage that lasted. But she wasn't a Colton or Bellamy or Maggie. She wasn't lucky or blessed.

But that was fine.

She didn't feel sorry for herself. She would just be happy that she had Forrest's protection. She wouldn't let herself hope for more—for his love.

As if he'd read her mind, Hays Colton told her, "Don't be afraid."

But was he talking about her hopes for his son? Or her fear for her life?

This was the first time he welcomed the unknown caller showing up on his cell phone screen. The first time he actually wanted to talk to the person who'd tried manipulating him into murder.

The murder of a man his daughter obviously loved.

The way she'd looked at Forrest Colton, with such concern, and at him, with such disgust, haunted Beau. He'd let her down. He knew that.

He'd let her down years ago.

But now…

Now he'd done more than disappoint her; he'd devastated her.

Guilt weighed heavily on him. A guilt that he knew he wouldn't be able to shake this time—not with the thrill of a bet or a drink or anything.

He'd screwed up too badly this time. He'd eluded arrest, assaulted not one but two police officers and he'd threatened his own daughter.

At least that was how she saw it. And now he saw himself through her eyes—as a pathetic excuse for a human being. He had to make this right.

Somehow.

So he clicked the accept button and before the man could berate him, he said, "I know I screwed up."

He wasn't sure how the hell this guy always knew, though. Did he have a police scanner? Some way of always knowing what was going on?

"What are you going to do about it?"

"I need to leave town," he said.

The guy chortled. "How the hell are you going to do that?"

"I've got some money stashed at my old house."

The guy snorted. "Yeah, right. If you had that, you would have paid me off right away."

"I didn't want you to know," he said. "I thought I could get rid of the detective, like you wanted, and save the money for myself."

"You're going to pay me off first," the guy replied, "before you go anywhere."

Beau smiled over what he heard in the guy's voice: greed. Beau understood it well. It was why—even when he was up—that he kept gambling. Because he wanted more.

This guy had to have money somehow—enough that he'd bought up Beau's debt. Yet he wanted more. Beau had been counting on it.

"My girl left the house," he said. "All the cops should be gone soon, too. I'm going to go back and get it. Then I'll bring it to you. Where can I meet you?"

And who the hell are you?

"I'll meet you," the man replied and clicked off the phone.

Beau uttered a shaky sigh. It was what he wanted. But he knew this was the most dangerous gamble he'd ever taken. This one could cost him his life.

Chapter 23

Forrest wanted to come inside the bedroom with her and take her into his arms—just to hold her, to comfort her. But he didn't trust himself to leave it at that, to leave her alone. And he hadn't told his parents how he felt about her, that he was doing more than protecting her. He was falling in love with her. Hell, he'd already fallen…hard.

"Do you have everything you need?" he asked from the doorway of the guest room next to the nursery. It would have been used for a nanny if his mother had ever had one to help with the boys. But she hadn't.

Rae grasped the baby monitor in her hand and nodded. "This was how I knew he was in there with Connor." She shuddered.

"I'm sorry," he said, guilt pressing heavily on him that he'd allowed the man to get into the house.

"It wasn't your fault," she said. "None of it was your fault. It was his. What would he have done to Connor if I hadn't heard him?"

Forrest had to reach out now, had to pull her trembling body against his chest to comfort her. "He wouldn't have hurt him."

She gently skimmed her fingertips along his swollen temple. "He hurt you." She shuddered. "And Officer Baker. He might have killed him."

Forrest shook his head. "No, he's going to be all right. Beau hasn't killed anyone."

But she pursed her lips as if she wasn't sure. "He admitted knowing that body had been buried in the backyard. How would he have known that?"

"The killer's been in contact with him," Forrest reminded her. So how did Beau not know his identity? Maybe the old gambler was better at bluffing than his debts would suggest. Maybe he did know.

Rae's brow furrowed with skepticism. "Yeah, right."

"You don't believe him?"

"I don't believe anything he says," she replied, and her voice cracked. "When Mom got sick, he said he would come back and that he would be a much better husband and father when he did. But he never came back, not even for her funeral."

Forrest's heart ached with her pain. He wanted to take it all away from her and give her nothing but love. He didn't know if she wanted that, though, or just the protection he'd promised her. He hadn't done the greatest job at keeping his promise, though. Her father had gotten inside the nursery, had gotten his hands on Connor.

But Forrest couldn't believe that he would have hurt his own grandson.

Rae sighed. "I'm sorry. All of that happened a long time ago. I should be over it now."

"His return brought all of those feelings back for you," Forrest surmised. "It must have been a shock to see him there." And he hadn't been there for her, hadn't protected her from that.

"It shouldn't have been," she said. "You were asking about him. You suspected it could have been him."

"I didn't really think he was the one threatening you and Connor," he admitted. Having been blessed with awesome parents himself, he couldn't imagine one of them threatening him or his child.

"You thought he was the killer," she said. "So why don't you think that anymore?"

He touched the bump on his head that still tingled from her fingertips sliding gently over it moments before. "He could have killed me."

"Maybe he thought he had," she suggested. "Maybe he didn't realize you weren't dead." Tears pooled in her eyes, revealing how hard it was for her to confront what her father could be: a killer.

"Stop," he told her. "Stop worrying about it, about him. Just get some rest."

Dark circles rimmed her big brown eyes as she stared up at him. There was something in her gaze besides worry and concern, something like what he was feeling. But was it real? Or was it only his wishful thinking putting it there?

He started leaning down, to look closer, to be closer.

He wanted to kiss her—needed to kiss her.

But the ringing of a phone drew him back to his senses. It wasn't his cell; it didn't even sound like a cell phone. His parents still had a landline, though, since the reception wasn't the greatest at the ranch.

Who would be calling at this time, though?

It was closer to dawn than midnight now. "Go to sleep," he urged her. "And maybe Connor will sleep in after tonight."

"I should stay in the nursery with him," she said with a worried glance at the closed door.

He wrapped his fingers around hers, which were wrapped around the baby monitor. "You have this. You'll hear him if he wakes up."

Just like she'd heard her father on the monitor.

She flinched, as if remembering that, and he wanted to hold her again, wanted to stay with her instead of going to his own room. As he opened his mouth to suggest it, he heard a creak on the stairs.

His hand went to his holster, and he whirled around to his father. "Just me," Hays Colton said as he held out a cordless phone toward him. "And I'm not sure who this is, but they want to speak with you."

Everybody with Whisperwood PD had his cell number. Who would be calling him here? And especially at this hour.

"Sorry, Dad," he said as he took the cordless from him.

His father offered a weary smile to him and to Rae. "It's never boring when you and your brothers are home," he said. He patted his son's broad shoulder. "And that's a good thing."

After all of the months he'd spent volunteering for desk duty with the Cowboy Heroes, Forrest would have agreed with him. He would have agreed if not for the danger Rae and Connor had been put in.

He turned back toward her. "Get some rest," he urged her. "I'll take this in my room." He forced himself to walk across the hall, to leave her alone.

She murmured a good-night to his father before stepping into the guest room and closing the door. Forrest did the same, stepping into his room and closing the door.

Then he raised the cordless phone to his face and asked, "Who is this?"

"It's Beau."

Despite his assurances to Rae that her father wasn't a killer, his blood chilled. The man must have been hiding in the shadows somewhere, must have overheard that Forrest was bringing the man's daughter and grandson back to the Colton ranch. Had he followed them?

Voices emanated from the baby monitor. But Rae knew the men who talked weren't in the nursery. She'd watched Forrest go to his bedroom. And the other man she could hear…

Forrest had assured her that he wouldn't get close to her again. Her father.

The baby monitor must have been on the same frequency as the cordless phone Forrest was using, because the reception was as clear as if they were on a conference call with Rae.

"Where are you?" Forrest asked her father.

"It doesn't matter where I am now," he replied. "It's where I'm going to be and who I'm meeting. You're going to want to be there, too."

"The killer?" Forrest asked, but there was skepticism in his voice now. He wasn't as convinced as he'd tried to sound to her that her father wasn't the murderer.

"Yes," Beau replied. "I tricked him into meeting me."

Was the killer whom he'd tricked, or was he trying now to trick Forrest?

Fear had her heart pounding furiously hard.

"Where?" Forrest asked.

"At my house," Beau replied.

And Rae bristled that he kept calling it that. He'd given it up years ago, when he'd left and never returned. It was hers now—her home and Connor's.

"You can't call in a bunch of police units, though," Beau warned him. "Or he'll get away before we get a chance to see who he is. You need to come alone."

And Rae's blood chilled. Was her father setting up the man she loved? Was he trying yet again to kill him?

She wanted to shout into the baby monitor. But she had the receiver, not the transmitter. They wouldn't hear her through it.

"When?" Forrest asked.

"Right away," Beau replied. "He should be here any minute now."

Forrest cursed. "You didn't give me enough damn time to get—"

"Just you," Beau warned. "Or you'll blow it."

And that was why he hadn't called sooner. He hadn't wanted to give Forrest time to call for backup.

"You can't call this in," Beau continued. "He might have someone within the department or be someone within the department. He knows too much."

Rae tossed the monitor down on the bed and rushed toward the door. When she pulled it open, Forrest was already in the hallway. She ran to him. "Don't go!"

He tensed. "What?"

"I heard the call—on the monitor," she said. "It's a trick."

He shook his head. "I don't think so."

"The killer—whoever he is—wants you not to work the murder cases," she reminded him. "This is how they're going to get rid of you." And her father was either going to help or do it himself. "Please don't go!"

She threw her arms around him, clinging to him, like she'd clung to her father when he'd headed out the door all those years ago. "Please…" Sobs cracked her voice.

As if he was in pain, Forrest grimaced. "I'm sorry, Rae. I have to."

She shook her head. "No, you don't. You can send someone else."

He shook his head now. "No. I won't put anyone else in danger."

"Then you know it's a trap," she said.

"I know it's my best chance of catching your father and finding the killer," he said. "I have to take it."

Her father had said something similar—whatever game he'd been leaving to play had been his best chance at changing their fortunes, at helping them.

"I'm doing it for you," Forrest said. "And for Connor."

She shuddered. "I didn't think you were anything like him," she said. "But you are. If you really cared about me and Connor, you wouldn't go. You wouldn't leave us."

"You're safe here," Forrest assured her.

"But you're not," she said. "You're rushing right into danger."

"That's my job," he reminded her. "It's what I do."

She pointed toward his bad leg. "It's what nearly got you killed. Is it worth it?"

"To stop killers and protect innocent people?" he asked. "Of course it's worth it." He pulled away from her then and headed toward the stairs, his limp even more pronounced than it usually was.

She couldn't help but think it would be the last time that she saw him. That he wouldn't come back to her.

Words burned in the back of her throat.

I love you.

She wanted to tell him. But would he stop? Would he believe her?

Would he care?

Despite his limp, he was already down the stairs. Then the door opened and closed as he left, taking her opportunity with him. She'd missed her chance to tell him how she felt about him. Would she have another opportunity?

Would she ever see him again?

His cell phone vibrated across his bedside table, and beside him in bed, Bellamy murmured in protest of the interruption of her sleep. She needed her rest.

So Donovan grabbed the phone and rushed out of the room. But when he stared down at the screen, he saw that he had two calls coming in at the same time.

Forrest and Rae.

Weren't they together?

What the hell was going on?

He hit a button and connected first with Forrest. "What—"

"Get out to the Lemmon house," Forrest ordered him.

"Is that why Rae's calling me, too?" Donovan asked. "Is she in danger?"

"No, she's at the ranch."

"Ranch?"

"Our ranch," Forrest said. "With Mom and Dad. She's safe."

Donovan's blood chilled. "But you're not."

And that was why Rae was calling him.

"I'm meeting her father there," Forrest said. "He's the one who ran me off the road and assaulted Officer Baker."

Donovan cursed. "That son of a bitch—"

"He's working for the real killer," Forrest said.

"Who—"

"He doesn't know," Forrest said. "That's why he's lured him back to Rae's—to find out."

It sounded more like he was luring Forrest there. "It's not safe," Donovan said.

He'd left his clothes and gun in the bedroom. But as much as he didn't want to wake Bellamy, he didn't want to lose his brother either. He had almost lost him once already. He rushed back in to grab his jeans and his holstered weapon.

"Wait for me," he said.

"I'm already here," Forrest said.

Before Donovan could say anything else, his brother disconnected the call. He'd gone in alone—without backup—just like the day he'd nearly died.

And Donovan couldn't help but think that this time Forrest might not make it.

Chapter 24

Forrest had a flashback to that day he'd walked into a warehouse to meet a potential witness and gunfire had erupted. He had nearly died that day.

The witness's call to meet had been a trap. This probably was, too. Just like Rae and Donovan had warned him.

But it was a risk he had to take if he wanted to make sure the nightmare for Rae and Connor ended, if he wanted to make sure they were safe. And they meant more to him than his own life.

He had to do this, had to take this risk.

He shut off the headlights as he approached her driveway. Even with the lights off, he didn't turn into the drive. Instead he parked his car on the side of the rural road. Before opening the driver's door, he pulled the fuse for the dome light. From that other trap, he'd learned not to announce his arrival.

And to be prepared. He drew his weapon. He'd been meant to die that day, but his shooter had been the one to die instead. He'd thought his life had ended then, too. But now he knew differently. He knew there was so much more to living than work. There was family.

He had a wonderful one.

But he wanted another one.

He wanted a family with Rae and Connor. The only way he'd have a chance of that, though, was to make sure they were no longer in danger.

To do that, he had to put himself in danger first. But would Rae forgive him for leaving after she had begged him to stay?

The only way he'd find out was if he survived this meeting. So he clasped his gun tightly in his hand as he headed toward the house. It was dark—all of the lights were off and the nursery window was boarded up.

Instead of walking down the driveway to the front porch, Forrest slipped around the back. The ground was uneven, causing him to stumble and nearly fall.

He swallowed a curse, not over the pain shooting up his bad leg but over the noise he might have made. He didn't want to alert anyone to his presence. Yet.

Was it just Beau here?

Or was the killer here, too?

Or were they one and the same?

He hoped not, because Beau knew this property too damn well. He'd already hidden on it too many times, with the police being unable to find him.

How would Forrest?

He knew one place where Beau kept turning up—at the grave he'd admitted to digging up. He'd turned up there to attack the young officer and to attack Forrest.

Forrest's head still pounded from the blow Beau had dealt him. If he returned to the site, he risked getting hurt worse. But it was a risk he had to take—for Rae and Connor.

Keeping to the shadows at the side of the house, Forrest headed around it, to the back. He flinched with every rustle of grass beneath his feet and every twig snapping under the heels of his boots. But then something drowned out the faint noises of his walking: an engine.

One revved in the driveway before tires squealed, and the noise grew fainter as the vehicle drove away. Had he been too late?

Had they already left?

Maybe Donovan had put in a call for backup, and like Beau had warned him, the killer had access to police dispatch. He cursed.

Another curse echoed his. But faintly.

Someone hadn't left. Someone else was hiding somewhere in the darkness.

Then a groan followed that curse, and Forrest pinpointed the direction of the sound. Just as he'd suspected, it came from the crime scene.

He rushed forward and noticed that the yellow tape no longer fluttered between two of those poles. It had snapped and now lay on the ground in two pieces. He stepped closer, his foot sinking into the loose soil. Then he peered into the hole.

And like he had twice before, he found another body. The first light of dawn illuminated the swollen face of the older man.

"Beau," Forrest called out.

"He's gone," the older man murmured. "You were too late."

Forrest scrambled down into the hole with him. As he did, he holstered his weapon and reached for his phone. "I'll get help…"

But Beau reached out and clasped his hand around the phone. "No."

"You're hurt."

"I'm dying," he said, his voice just a husky rasp.

As the light grew, Forrest could see the marks around his neck, too. He'd been strangled like the other victims.

"You can survive this," Forrest assured him.

Beau used his other hand to gesture toward his chest and to the end of the pipe sticking out between his ribs.

Forrest flinched and cursed. The pain had to be intolerable. And the strength of the killer…

"Who is he?" Forrest asked. "Who did this to you?"

Beau shook his head. "No."

"You saw him," Forrest said. "You had to see him."

"I did," Beau acknowledged. "But I made a deal."

"A deal with a killer?" His killer—because Beau was right. He was dying. There was no way he could survive with the blood gurgling out around the pipe shoved deep within his body. Not even if Forrest called for help.

"He won't hurt Rae and the baby if I don't say who he is."

"And you trust him?" Forrest asked.

Beau just stared up at him.

"You trust him?" Forrest repeated.

Then he realized that Beau couldn't see him or hear him anymore. He was gone.

But Forrest wasn't alone. Dirt sifted down into the hole as someone approached it, and a dark shadow fell across him and the dead man.

He'd thought the killer had left, but maybe when he'd seen Forrest's SUV parked on the road, he'd circled back to finish off him like he'd done Beau.

He reached for his holster to draw his weapon. But another gun already cocked. And he had no doubt it was aimed at his head. He wouldn't be able to shoot his way out of this trap, like he had his last one.

After Forrest had left, Rae hadn't even tried to sleep. She'd known it would be no use—not with Forrest out there, alone. No. He wasn't alone.

When Donovan had returned her missed call, he'd been on his way to her house to meet Forrest. But Forrest had left long before he had. He would have already been there. He would have already walked into whatever trap her father had set for him.

Tears stung her eyes, and she stared down at Connor with blurred vision. She cradled the sleeping baby as she rocked in the chair she'd found in the nursery. Probably the same chair in which Josephine Colton had rocked all of her children.

How could her father be such a monster? How could he have threatened her and Connor and tried to kill officers of the law? And the man she loved.

Of course he didn't know she'd fallen for Forrest Colton. Forrest didn't know either. She should have told him when the words had been burning the back of her throat.

She should have told him then, because now she might never get the chance to tell him that she loved him. She blinked and focused on Connor.

Forrest was so good with him, so gentle, like he was with her. He was a good man.

That was why he'd insisted on leaving, on putting his life in danger. Because he was a good man, intent on taking care of everyone else before himself.

The one person he'd thought would take care of him had taken off when he'd needed her most. Rae couldn't understand how the woman he'd loved could have abandoned him. She couldn't understand how anyone could abandon him.

She should have chased him down the stairs, should have insisted on going along with him. Maybe her father wouldn't have hurt him if she'd been present. But knowing how protective Forrest was, she knew he wouldn't have allowed it. He would never willingly put her in danger.

Just himself.

It was his job.

Could she live with that, if he lived? Could she live with his putting himself in danger over and over again?

Because every time he left the house for his job, he might wind up leaving her forever.

That was why she'd chosen not to wait for a man to start her family. Her dating history had proved to her that she had her mother's luck with choosing men; she picked ones who couldn't commit for life.

Forrest Colton had no problem with committing. His problem was that he was committed most to his job. His dangerous job. And that commitment might have gotten him killed.

He'd been gone so long. He'd left when it was dark, and now the sun had risen, pouring light and warmth into the already-sunny yellow nursery.

She'd heard footsteps earlier. People moving around the house—probably Forrest's parents. How worried were they? How did they handle all of their children being in dangerous professions?

How would she handle it if Connor someday chose a high-risk career?

She gazed down at him with such awe, wondering what kind of man he would become. He had her father's genes in him. Would that make him a gambler? And selfish?

But he had her mother's and hers as well, so maybe he would be kind and generous and hardworking. What he needed, she realized now, was a strong male role model.

A man like Forrest.

Who put other people's safety before his own. It was noble. For him.

But so damn hard on those who loved him, like she did.

The doorbell pealed, the bell a faint tinkle this far from the front door. The nursery faced the front of the house, where the driveway was.

Lifting Connor, she carried him to the window and peered out. An SUV was parked on the driveway, with lights fastened to the roof of it. An officer stood beside the driver's door, while the passenger's door was already open.

Forrest wouldn't have rung the bell for his own house. The visitor had to be someone else—the chief, no doubt.

Wouldn't he be the one who made the notification when one of his officers was killed in the line of duty?

Was that what he'd come here to do—notify Forrest's parents that he was gone?

This was the worst damn part of his job. The chief hated making notifications. Hell, he shouldn't even be doing this one. He'd been asked not to, but he figured she had a right to know as soon as possible…in case she wanted to see his body before they took him away.

When the door opened, it was Hays who stood in front of him. Dark circles rimmed his eyes, and he looked tense with worry. "Archer, it's early for a visit."

Hays was a rancher; he'd probably been up for a while. It wasn't the hour he was questioning, but it was the purpose.

"I'm here to see Ms. Lemmon," he told his old friend.

Hays sucked in a breath. Then, his jaw taut, he asked, "About my son?"

Archer furrowed his brow with confusion. "Forrest wanted to do this himself." And now he understood why; the single mom was more than someone the detective was protecting. She was important to him.

When she rushed down the steps to greet him, it was clear from the fear on her face that Forrest was important to her, too.

"Is he all right?" she asked. Tears already streamed down her face with the emotion overwhelming her. "Is he?"

Were her tears for her father, though, or for Forrest? Archer wasn't sure now who she was upset about.

But he began his notification as he always did, "I'm sorry for your loss."

And a small scream slipped through her lips as she slipped to the floor. Hays was there, with his arm around her, lifting her back up, letting her lean against him. The Coltons were good people, important people in Whisperwood.

But that wasn't why the chief felt so damn bad about being here. He felt bad for Rae Lemmon. The young woman had already lost so much.

"Your father, Beau Lemmon, died earlier this morning," Archer continued.

Rae gasped again. "My father?"

"Yes, you were aware that he'd returned to town." At least that was what Forrest had told him.

She jerked her chin in a sharp nod. "Yes, he was the one threatening me and my son."

Hays tightened his arm around her. "I'm sorry, honey," he murmured.

"And Forrest," she continued. "He tried to kill Forrest." Her voice cracked. "How is he?"

She was obviously afraid that she'd lost him, too. She wasn't the only one who was afraid of that. Archer wondered himself.

Chapter 25

Forrest had been gone too long. He knew it. But he'd wanted to make sure he—and the crime-scene techs—didn't miss a single clue that might lead them to the killer of the women and of Beau Lemmon.

He hoped like hell they would find some DNA, something that would lead them to the real monster. Beau Lemmon hadn't been a monster. He'd just been—as Rae had once said—flawed.

How was she?

She hadn't returned to her house with the chief like he'd thought she might. But then, after what had happened at her house, would she ever want to come home to it?

He didn't want her to—he didn't want her here, where so many terrible things had happened. Hell, he could have died here himself when Beau had struck him over the head, and just a few hours ago when that gun had cocked.

Fortunately it had been his brother holding the weapon, and not the murderer. Donovan hadn't recognized him right away, crouched in the shadows of the old grave. And the new one.

It had become Beau Lemmon's grave. His body was gone now, though. And that was why Forrest had finally left to return to the ranch. When he drove up, he found his parents on the porch. His mother held Connor in her lap as she rocked in the swing, while his father leaned against the railing beside them, making faces at the baby.

Warmth spread through Forrest's chest. He loved the two of them so much. "Babysitting?" he teased.

"Heard you've been doing some of this yourself," his father mused with a curious glance at him.

They knew. They knew he'd fallen for the baby and his sweet single mother. He didn't bother denying it; he just grinned at them.

"Your services might no longer be required," his father said.

And Forrest furrowed his brow. "You threatening to take over my job?"

"We're only watching him while Rae gathers up his stuff," his mother said, with disappointment heavy in her voice. "She's leaving."

Forrest cursed and then shook his head. He had to remember not to swear in front of the baby. Eventually Connor would be repeating words. But Forrest might not be around anymore when he did—if Rae had her way, apparently. She'd been mad when he'd left last night. She was probably furious that the chief—not he—had done the notification.

"Is she okay?" he asked.

"You would know better than we would," Hays remarked with a curious glance.

They had their suspicions about his relationship with Rae, but apparently they didn't know if it was going to last. Neither did he.

He'd been such an idiot by fighting his feelings like he had, thinking that she was anything like Shannon. Rae wasn't the kind who took off.

Or she hadn't been.

When he rushed up the steps, he found her in the nursery, packing, just as his parents had warned him. "So you're the one leaving now," he mused.

She didn't look up, but she tensed. "There's no reason to stay."

"No reason?" he asked. Didn't she feel the same way about him that he did about her?

"My father is dead," she said, her voice curiously flat and emotionless. But when she lifted her face to meet his gaze, her eyes were red and swollen. She'd been crying.

And he hadn't been here to hold her, to comfort her. Guilt squeezed his heart in a tight grip. "I'm sorry," he murmured. "I was too late to save him."

"You shouldn't have gone at all," she said, her voice cracking now as her emotions rushed back. "You could have died with him."

He shook his head. "I've been doing this a long time," he reminded her. "I'm a good cop." Even with his disability. The chief was giving him a chance to prove it. Now he just had to find the killer.

With so many of his family members working the case now, it was just a matter of time before the killer was caught and brought to justice for all of his crimes.

"He was tricking you," she said.

Forrest shook his head. "No. He was trying to help me."

She snorted. "Yeah, right. Did he tell you who the killer was?"

He shook his head again. "No. But he kept that secret for you," he told her. "He made a deal with the killer that he'd keep quiet if the guy left you and Connor alone."

"So then Connor and I absolutely can go home," she said. "Alone." She drew in a deep breath. "We don't need you anymore."

He sucked in a breath of his own, but just to brace himself for the rejection that was probably to come. She was furious with him, and for good reason. He'd left just like her father had—when she'd begged him not to go.

And he hated himself for it. Not nearly as much as she apparently hated him, though.

"I need you," he said. "I need you and I need Connor."

She narrowed her eyes with suspicion. "Why?"

"Because I love you," he said. "I love you both. You're the reasons I left last night—you and Connor. I wanted to make sure you'd be safe. You two mean *everything* to me. And if you give me the chance, I will prove that to you. I will never, ever leave you again."

Rae didn't say anything. She just turned and ran from the room. Ran away just like Shannon had.

Maybe he was just that unlovable.

Rae was too overwhelmed to speak. Emotions rushed through her—relief, fear and a love so powerful that she wasn't sure how to handle it. If she could handle it.

And that was why she was so afraid.

But she could trust Forrest. He was nothing like her father. But if she believed what Forrest had told her, her father had come through in the end. His very last act in life had finally been a selfless one.

Tears stung her eyes, so when she turned back toward the room in which Forrest stood, she could barely see him. But his shoulders were slumped with exhaustion and maybe disappointment.

She hadn't handled his proposal well—if that was what that had been. "Aren't you coming?" she asked him.

He turned toward her now, his brow furrowed with confusion. And she held out her hand to him. He moved slowly, his limp more pronounced than she'd seen it since he'd been in the car accident.

But that hadn't been an accident.

"Were you hurt last night?" she asked with concern.

"Not last night," he replied as he joined her in the hallway.

She'd hurt him just now. "I'm sorry," she said. "It's just so hard for me to believe."

"What is?" he asked.

"That you love me."

He moved faster now, across the hall. He pushed open his bedroom door, then reached back and pulled her inside with him. "Why is that hard to believe? Don't you know how amazing you are?"

A smile tugged at her lips.

"You're beautiful and smart and so damn loyal and generous and—"

She rose on tiptoe and pressed her mouth to his, shutting off his words. She kissed him with all of the desperation she'd felt the night before, with all of the fear and the love she hadn't let herself express.

He pulled back, panting for breath, and murmured, "Do you believe me? Do you believe that I love you?"

She could see it in his face now, in his warm gaze and in the tentative smile that curved his lips. "Yes," she said. "And I love you, too. So much." The emotion overwhelmed her. "I wanted to tell you last night. I should have told you. If something had happened to you…" Tears stung her eyes, making her nose wrinkle.

He leaned down and kissed it. "Nothing happened to me. And I don't think anything will happen to you or Connor now either. But I still want us to be careful. To stay here."

"Will your parents be okay with that?" she asked. "We're not imposing?" She'd felt guilty for having them watch Connor while she'd packed up his stuff.

He chuckled. "Are you kidding? They're both doting on their new grandson right now."

"New grandson?"

"That's how they see Connor already," Forrest said. "That's how I see him, too—as my son. I hope you'll let me adopt him and make it official."

Her heart felt as if it would burst, it swelled with so much love. She'd wanted Connor to have a father someday—a father like Forrest, whom he could count on. But grandparents…?

She hadn't even thought about everything her son hadn't had—until he had it now. "Thank you," she said. "Thank you for being the most amazing man."

He shook his head. "I'm not the best bet, you know," he warned her. And she could see the seriousness in his eyes now, the doubt and fear. "I may not be able to get another job because of my disability. I may not be able to play with Connor like I'd want—"

She pressed her lips to his again to stop his words and to show her love. But then she pulled back and assured him, "You're a hero, Forrest Colton. You've saved us so many times, and not just physically. You've saved me emotionally. I was scared to open up my heart, to trust anyone. I'm not a gambler like my father. But you're not a bet. You're a sure thing."

He smiled again. "We're a sure thing."

"Yes, we are."

He lifted her then and carried her the few steps to his bed. It might have been his old room, but thankfully it wasn't a twin-size bed but a four-poster king-size one. The mattress dipped beneath their weight as he joined her. Clothes were tugged off or pushed aside until they were together again, their bodies joined like their hearts and souls.

Rae had never felt anything as right—as perfect—as making love with Forrest Colton. They knew instinctively how to move, where to touch, where to kiss…

He drove her crazy with his lips and his fingertips. And she returned the favor with hers. They moved faster and faster, with perspiration wetting their skin and tension building inside them. Then finally it broke within Rae—pleasure shuddering through her. She cried out his name before burying her face in his neck. His body tensed beneath hers. He gripped her hips and drove a little deeper into her before his pleasure filled her. He groaned and released a cry of his own. Her name.

"I love you," he said. "So damn much."

She smiled. "You don't sound too thrilled about it."

"I'm kicking myself for the weeks I wasted," he said. "I should have said yes when you asked me to dance at the wedding."

"Why didn't you?" she wondered.

"I thought you were just feeling sorry for me."

And his pride wouldn't have been able to handle that.

"Not at all," she assured him. "I thought you were handsome and so alone…" And she'd been so alone then, too, despite having just given birth to Connor the month before.

"We're not going to be alone ever again," he promised her. "We will always have each other."

She hadn't believed she'd ever find a love like that for herself. A love like the Coltons had. But now she knew it was possible—because she'd fallen for a Colton, and soon she and Connor would become Coltons, too.

A promise was a promise.

Usually he wouldn't have worried about keeping one. But Beau Lemmon had died without revealing his identity. So maybe laying off the guy's kid and grand-kid was the right thing to do—to hold up his side of that promise.

And hell, they were the best distraction to keep the Austin detective from working his cases. He'd fallen so hard for them that he was going to stick close, even if they were no longer in danger.

But that didn't mean they'd stay safe. Promise be damned, nobody was safe…if they got too close to fig-uring out who he was…

* * * * *

Don't miss the next story in the exciting
Colton 911 series:

Colton 911: Target in Jeopardy
by Carla Cassidy

Available September 2019 from
Harlequin Romantic Suspense!

"You're scaring me."

"I'm sorry. I don't mean to. I just have something to tell you that I think you'd want to know."

"Are you leaving Santa Raquel?"

"Make the call, Miranda. Please?"

Less than a minute later, she had him back on the phone. "All set. You want to go to my place?"

"No. And not mine, either. You know that car dealership out by the freeway?" He named a cash-for-your-car type of lot. One that didn't ask many questions if you had enough money, which made her even more uneasy.

"Yeah."

What was he doing? What could he possibly have to say?

Unless he'd found out who was watching her...

"Head over there," he told her. "I'll be right behind you."

"You're sure I'm safe?"

"Yes."

"You're really scaring me now, Tad."

"Call Chantel," he said. "She'll assure you that my request is valid."

"You've talked to her today?"

"I had to tell her I wouldn't be at the High Risk meeting."

Oh. So he was leaving. Which didn't explain why she was on her way to a car lot.

And suddenly she didn't want to know. Life without Tad was inevitable. But did it have to happen right now? When the rest of her world could be caving in?

Don't miss
Her Detective's Secret Intent *by Tara Taylor Quinn,*
available September 2019 wherever
Harlequin® *Romantic Suspense books*
and ebooks are sold.

www.Harlequin.com

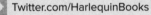

Love Harlequin romance?

DISCOVER.

Be the first to find out about promotions, news and exclusive content!

 Facebook.com/HarlequinBooks

 Twitter.com/HarlequinBooks

Instagram.com/HarlequinBooks

Pinterest.com/HarlequinBooks

ReaderService.com

EXPLORE.

Sign up for the Harlequin e-newsletter and download a free book from any series at **TryHarlequin.com.**

CONNECT.

Join our Harlequin community to share your thoughts and connect with other romance readers!
Facebook.com/groups/HarlequinConnection

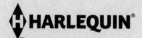

**ROMANCE WHEN
YOU NEED IT**

HSOCIAL2018

Reward the book lover in you!

Earn points on your purchase of new Harlequin books from participating retailers.

Turn your points into **FREE BOOKS** of your choice!

Join for FREE today at
www.HarlequinMyRewards.com.

Harlequin My Rewards is a free program (no fees) without any commitments or obligations.

MYR18